I0547762

The Angel's Trumpet

Portia of the Pacific

Volume 4

JAMES MUSGRAVE

ISBN: 978-1-943457-39-7

Published by EMRE Publishing Fiction
San Diego, CA

"James Musgrave's *The Angel's Trumpet* is one of those rare historical mysteries that is both entirely plausible and yet truly original. A richly researched adventure into the complex social web of Gilded Age Washington, featuring deeply-realized and re-imagined luminaries including actress Sarah Bernhardt and President and Mrs. Cleveland, the novel is also surprisingly modern in its sensibilities, a compelling romp into an earlier era's struggle with addiction and vice and secrecy and race relations, and, most of all, hidden sources of power. You will read this book in one sitting--and you will be very glad that you did. A meticulously-plotted gem from a master of the genre."

--Jacob M. Appel, Esq., Winner of the Dundee International Novel Award for *The Man Who Wouldn't Stand Up.*

"The Angel's Trumpet has as many twists and turns as an Alpine highway, and I thoroughly enjoyed the trip. The story, set in Washington D. C. during the Grover Cleveland administration, provides a marvelous insight into the societal interaction of the times as well as the interactions between the races. The characters are intense and the action riveting. It's one of those books that when you pick it up you can't put it down until you've finished it."

--Philip Mintz, Esq., Screenwriter and former attorney

"The way Musgrave weaves together real-life characters in fictional settings reminds me of *Ragtime.* I think in this novel in this series Musgrave comes closest to recreating the period of Reconstruction. I am able to visualize in my mind Washington DC of the late 19th century, a period that laid the foundation of the Jim Crow era. My favorite character is Sarah Bernhardt. Musgrave is able to peel away the trappings of fame and fortune that embodied this period to reveal not only a skilled actress but a very vulnerable and maternal figure. She is David's 'real mother.' I think readers will readily see the parallels the Gilded Age have with our plutocratic riddled world today and white nationalism. Musgrave is really an amazing writer."

--Matteo Lesser, PhD, Professor of American Studies

The Angel's Trumpet

By

James Musgrave

© 2019 by James Musgrave

Published by English Majors, Reviewers and Editors, LLC

An English Majors, Reviewers and Editors Book Copyright 2019

English Majors, Reviewers and Editors Publishers is a publishing house based in San Diego, California.

Website: emrepublishing.com

For more information, please contact:

English Majors, Reviewers and Editors, LLC

DEDICATION

To those citizens of the world who continue to be unafraid of differences, who worship the environment rather than the accumulation of wealth, and who understand the importance of keeping an open mind toward all human endeavors.

Other Works by This Author

The Portia of the Pacific Historical Mysteries

Interactive and Multimedia Enhanced eBooks

EMRE Publishing is now selling completely "enhanced" versions of its books through the unique Embellisher Multimedia Stream platform. Simply register inside the eReader to have access to the variety of titles. They contain relevant historical videos, music, interactive content, and a complete audiobook edition in many of the great titles.

Visit https://emrepublishing.com/new_embellisher-ereader/ to see what's available. In addition, if you are also an author or one who sells online, you may want to take Professor Musgrave's free online course, "Developing Your Digital Marketing Platform" (https://payhip.com/b/j3Xs). Besides eBooks, you will learn how to sell other tangible goods and services, as well as digital podcasts, courses, and a variety of video products.

"Find out just what any people will quietly submit to and you have the exact measure of the injustice and wrong which will be imposed on them."
—Frederick Douglass

"Regard your soldiers as your children, and they will follow you into the deepest valleys. Look on them as your own beloved sons, and they will stand by you even unto death!"
—Sun Tzu

"They called me the lady lawyer … a dainty sobriquet … that enabled me to maintain a dainty manner, as I browbeat my way through the marshes of ignorance and prejudice."
—Clara Shortridge Foltz, Esq.

Table of Contents

Chapter 1: Suffragette

Swampoodle Grounds, Washington, D. C., May 4, 1887.

Eloise Strong, at twenty-four, knew that her time was precious. She must obtain a recommendation from her lover, Marshal Owens, or she would never be admitted to law school. As she pushed and shoved her way through the crowds assembled at the ball park, her eyes focused on him, the tall red-haired gentleman standing near the Nationals' bench.

The Washington team was playing the Detroit Wolverines, who were in first place, so the stands were filled with a raucous assortment of cheering men. There was only one man Eloise wanted to see, and she was almost up to him when she felt a hand pulling on her left arm.

"Miss? Where do you think you're going?" A tall bearded man, in a maroon frock coat and striped britches, whose breath smelled of onion and garlic, was scowling down at her. He wore a black bowler with a scarlet cobra badge on the front. This meant he was one of the toughs who protected the illegal gambling going on amongst the mostly male spectators. Eloise assumed he was a gangster of some kind.

"I must talk to this gentleman," she said, pointing toward Marshal, who was now turning toward her, a confused look on his face under his brown gentleman's derby with the tiny pheasant feather in the band. Her lover was wearing brown corduroy trousers, and a matching topcoat, with a green velvet vest and a mink collar. He tugged at his reddish-brown, walrus mustache, which Eloise knew was a signal that he was quite irritated.

"What are you doing here?"

Marshal's fifty-five years showed in his wrinkled forehead and crow's feet, as he frowned at her. Eloise wondered why white men aged faster.

"May we talk?"

She took his arm. He had always been easy to persuade, from

the first time she ushered him into the upper bedrooms of the Oyster Glen Restaurant on Massachusetts, where she worked.

They walked toward the Refreshment Tents, over by the first base side of the field.

Eloise knew Marshal was an Appellate Court Judge. He had never kept his professional life secret from her, and this was the main reason she was there. She had a unique chance to enroll in Harvard Law School, as its first Negro woman, but she needed his recommendation to allow her to bypass the usual scrutiny. Marshal had often remarked upon her astute legal mind, and he had encouraged her education, even if it had started late.

As they strolled into the shade of the tents, she could smell the odors of popped corn, oysters on the half shell, and grilled chicken and frankfurters.

"We had a guest speaker in Mrs. Terrell's class today. He plays in the International League for the Newark club. Moses Fleetwood Walker. Do you know him?"

She wanted to get Marshal in a good mood, and she knew he loved baseball.

"Yes. I do. There are still a few Negroes playing in that league. That will all be changing, however, at the end of this season."

He took out one of his Cuban cigars from the breast pocket of his top coat, bit off the end, and spat it onto the sawdust. The deep tone of Marshal's voice sounded negative as he lit his smoke and began to puff.

"The owners have informed us they will be preventing any race-mixing on teams beginning next season. Except for a few star players, who shall be grandfathered with old contracts, no new Negro will be allowed to play."

Eloise reached into her blue handbag and rummaged around for something. When she found it, she turned to face him. She watched, as his deep blue, privileged Welsh eyes roamed freely over her body.

She wore the new powder blue dress from Paris, with its tiny straw hat and blue satin band, and the matching handbag with silver clasps. He bought it for her on their anniversary. It had been a passionate relationship of fifteen months, filled with clandestine meetings in various hotels around Washington, but they had never, until that moment, been seen together in public.

"Mr. Walker will want to know that. He seemed to be optimistic about the future of our race in baseball. The sport, he said, was one of the few fields of endeavor where performance mattered more than birth privilege." She saw him smile, so she continued. "Except, he said, many of the white Southern boys seem to enjoy sliding into his catcher position at home plate with their metal cleats brandished like Confederate swords."

Marshal reached out to touch Eloise on her slender, alabaster nose, and moved down to caress his index finger on her equally thin pink lips. "Your genetics, thank goodness, allow you to mix rather well with the public." He reached around her head and grasped a lock of her tight black curls. "Except for your hair, which has also been grandfathered in, it seems."

"Has the Attorney General summoned you yet? The *Post* had an editorial by President Cleveland about why he chose you for the Supreme Court. Mrs. Terrell read it to our class. I was so proud of you!"

She brought her right hand out of the handbag and thrust it inside the crook of his left forearm, holding it there, her brown eyes gazing up at his face.

"What was it you wanted to ask?" Marshal gently took her arm away, and it fell limply to her side. "Honestly, my dear, it's rather reckless of us to be seen out here." He swiveled his head, from side-to-side, searching for anyone he recognized in the crowd.

"Why dangerous? You're known to be one of Washington's most available bachelors. You said I was equal to any woman you've ever met, in both intelligence and beauty."

Eloise recalled their long embraces and his frequent promises of adoration. Now, however, something had changed in his eyes. It was as if their long talks together had meant nothing.

Her lover bent forward, cupped his right hand up to his mouth, and whispered. She could feel the spray from his lips upon

3

her cheeks. "I shall be on the highest court in the land. I cannot be seen with a bastard and former slave. Your outward appearance means nothing to those in my social circle. It is your breeding that matters. Just like your friend, Fleetwood Walker. There can be no more contracts with the major leagues, no matter how well you both play the game."

Her right hand, once more, reached down into her handbag. As her gaze riveted onto his, she could envision Moses Walker's face, as it superimposed over this stranger, this imposter lover.

Walker's lean, dark, and intelligent face, with flaring, wide nostrils, sensitive and bountiful lips, spoke the words she remembered. His father was a physician, a respected medical doctor. Eloise could hear his carefully enunciated speech coming from beneath that perfectly groomed mustache. What he had spoken in class now made this white man's swollen pink jowls and ugly scowl seem ludicrous in the bright sunshine.

Social inequality means that in all the relations that exist between man and man he is to be measured and taken not according to his natural fitness and qualification, but that blind and relentless rule, which accords certain pursuits and certain privileges to origin or birth.

When she finally spoke, her words sounded hollow and without passion.

"I can be accepted into Harvard Law School, where you graduated, Marshal. I simply need a single letter of recommendation. That's what Mr. Terrell told me. He, too, graduated from Harvard, and he believes I can be the first Negro woman to attend. Won't you allow me this chance? Doesn't our love, for all these months, mean anything to you?"

When Marshal began to lecture her, Eloise began to fantasize. She had done this many times before in her life. After the Civil War, in Virginia, she was eight years old, working in the plantation tobacco fields as an emancipated slave and sharecropper. A white man came riding up on a black horse and addressed all of the workers, telling them they could live free and get free schooling in the nation's capital. She had dreamed then, along with the others, and so they made the journey across the Potomac and into the city. She had no other hope, as her mother had died during child birth, the year before, and her father, and former master, Patrick Sloan Wolsey, sold his property and moved to Texas, the last location of the Confederacy, before the war ended.

". . . and I can no longer see you. My responsibilities are to this great nation of ours, and my reputation is at stake . . ."

Marshal's voice continued to drone, on and on, just the way Mr. and Mrs. Terrell's voices had done, promising her that she could rise up, and become educated, in order to demonstrate to those powerful elite that freedom extended to those who advanced through hard work and study. Her sympathetic tears agreed with the fantasies of her elders, and they flooded her mind, blotting-out the reality of her daily life. She did work hard, she studied hard, and she improved her lot, even though she had to do it by selling her body to the prominent politicians who frequented the restaurant where she worked as a waitress.

". . . Attorney General Garland chose me because I was independent. I cannot become encumbered with the likes . . ."

Eloise tightened her grip on the object inside her handbag. The Preparatory High School for Negroes was also selling her a dream. She was the only one of those from the plantation who had tested high enough to gain entrance. Even so, she had to become a prostitute to earn sufficient money to stay in school. And now, the biggest fantasy of all had come into her life: the idea that she, a half-Negro and half-woman, could gain access to the most prestigious university in the world. All she needed was a single, signed letter from a white judge. The key to her future, the gentleman standing in front of her, lecturing her, telling her about the reality of this nation's collective dream, had become, for her, an existential nightmare.

He was now smiling, reaching out once more, to touch her lips with his white forefinger, and she fantasized about the painting on the wall of the Sistine Chapel she had seen in one of her textbooks. It was created by the Italian artist, Michelangelo, and the metaphor now seemed very prophetic to her. The naked white man, Adam, was reaching out to touch the white-bearded, white God's finger. And she, a woman who was also white, but in color only, was now being touched by a man who was her new master. But she had this master in her web.

Her eyes moved down to Marshal's chest. The dagger inside her handbag was released from its feminine lair, so she dropped the bag, and she thrust its silver blade, glinting wildly in the sunlight, into this Man-god's heart-of-no-heart. She kept her unwavering fist around the dagger's black handle, as he bled all over her forearm, and it was her turn to smile.

She could feel the last pulsations of his heart's dark chambers, vibrating on the dagger's handle, as the masculine crowd around her circled the falling man, who was now on his knees. She bent over with him, as he collapsed backward onto the sawdust, writhing in pain like a serpent, his derby rolling away. She kept her right hand glued upon the hilt of the dagger, until Marshal made his final, gasping argument on this Earth, to the gathered throng of sportsmen and gawkers encircling him.

"Why, Eloise? You are now doomed."

Chapter 2: Mulatto's Life

The Hopkins Mansion, One Nob Hill, San Francisco, May 4, 1887.

C lara was supervising the packing for her trip to Washington, D. C. The information she received from the Attorney General's Office about the assassination was not detailed, but it was enough to get her mind working on a possible defense.

Mrs. Miriam Levine, Attorney General Augustus Hill Garland's assistant, was working for the White House, back in 1884, when she came to San Francisco to confront Clara during the Chinatown murders case. She was very kind to provide the attorney with the basic information about the arrest and the charges brought against Miss Eloise Strong, the accused murderess.

Clara was going over what she had in writing, as her next-to-youngest child, fifteen-year-old David Milton, meticulously organized her luggage. She promised she would take him with her to Washington, for educational purposes, and he was quite elated, whistling as he packed her shoes in their holders.

She was worried about him, however. He had recently begun to demonstrate more signs of effeminate behavior. Trella Evelyn caught him trying on one of her dresses, and he was a walking encyclopedia of knowledge about the French actress, Sarah Bernhardt. His present goal was to help Clara on a case so he could portray a female in "disguise."

David had always been more introverted and shier as a child. He had taken the desertion of his father, Civil War vet Jerimiah Foltz, especially hard. She almost had to force-feed him, he was so despondent and grief-stricken. When he began playing with dolls and creating impromptu theater displays, his mood improved, and this interest in theatrics and Romantic literature continued into his teen years.

Clara had consulted her mental professional friends, Elizabeth Packard and Dr. Andrew McFarland, who had assisted her inside the Stockton State Insane Asylum during their recent investigation. They assured her that her son did not have a mental disease, as they believed the teachings of the new psychoanalyst, Sigmund Freud. Dr. Freud believed humans were innately bisexual and that homosexuality was a conditioned behavior.

They also knew about the so-called "mental health aversion therapies" that were being promoted. The aversions included patients being given chemicals that made them vomit when they, for example, looked at photos of their lovers. Other homosexuals were being given electrical shocks—sometimes to their genitals—while they looked at homosexual pornography or cross-dressed. Both Packard and McFarland suggested that she simply monitor David's activities and not show concern, unless he became depressed.

She found out from Mrs. Levine that the Attorney General, Augustus Garland, was going to personally try the prosecution's case. She knew he was the first Southern Democrat to be appointed to a Cabinet position, and her attorney friend, Laura de Force Gordon, was busy doing research on him. As for the alleged assassination murder, there were dozens of eye-witnesses at the scene, as it had occurred in the middle of a professional baseball game. The weapon, a six-inch silver dagger, was in Eloise's hand when they pulled it out of the victim's chest and heart. The accused had been a student at the Preparatory School for Negroes, and she also worked at the Oyster Glen Restaurant and Tavern on Massachusetts Avenue. Clara would be able to speak with her client at the women's section of the D. C. Central Detention Facility at 1901 D Street, Southeast.

She knew she would need to question many people in this case, as this was going to be one of the most reported trials ever conducted. As a result, she planned to take with her Laura Gordon and Captain of Detectives, Isaiah Lees, who were going to serve on her legal defense team.

In addition, Dr. Andrew McFarland had agreed to examine Eloise Strong in his expert capacity as the Superintendent and Chief Physician of the Oak Lawn Retreat in Illinois, a private mental hospital. Of course, there was also David Milton, who was presently holding one of her orange frocks up to his chest and admiring it in the dressing mirror of the bedroom.

"David. Sweetheart. Don't fuss with my attire. I'll need those for court."

She was happy that Dr. McFarland was going to be there. Perhaps he could shed more light on Dr. Freud and his theories so she could understand what to expect from her son.

"Mother? Did you know that the Divine Sarah was a bastard? Just like the woman you're going to be defending. Miss Bernhardt was the illegitimate daughter of a Jewish lady named Judith who had established herself in France. Judith was a courtesan and was just sixteen when Sarah was born."

She smiled. "That's quite interesting, David. Remember Dr. McFarland? He's going to be there with us. We will certainly be exploring the background and childhood of our client. It's our job as the defense counsel to understand the extenuating circumstances that may have contributed to her outrageous act against Justice Owens."

David's eyes widened, and she knew he was now competing with his siblings for her attention. Samuel, Trella Evelyn, and Bertha May had all played important parts in her three previous cases. This was David's turn to shine.

"Should you attempt a plea of insanity the good doctor will be an excellent resource. If you need me to portray a Negro student, I would prefer to wear female attire along with my coloring."

David spun around with one of her dresses held in front of his thin body.

"How do I look?"

"Quite grand, indeed. However, I don't believe we shall be planting any incognito spies this time around. You can help me the most by engaging my mind with your excellent argumentative skills."

When David looked downcast, she remembered what Dr. McFarland said about depression.

"Of course, your acting skills *are* sublime. And, if we do need a spy, you shall be the first person I will seek out."

As her son completed his meticulous packing chore,

performing some particularly mesmerizing dancing as he did so, she began to think about the motives the Attorney General and, quite possibly, President Cleveland had for choosing her as the defense attorney.

It was becoming common knowledge in California and throughout the United States that she was a supporter of women's and minority rights, and her plan to create a state public defender's office was also part of her current efforts. Perhaps Garland and Cleveland simply believed Eloise Strong stood the best chance with her as defense attorney; but, the more realistic premise stood out in her mind. Every courtroom case she had argued thus far had been lost. Therefore, if these men wanted to push for a first-degree murder conviction, who better to oppose them than a three-time loser such as Clara Shortridge Foltz? It was this train of thought that made her angry. She was so angry, in fact, that she made a promise to herself to use every avenue of subterfuge, every possible ruse and trick, in order to keep her client's lovely neck out of the hangman's noose.

"Hello, Clara. Are you about ready? I have more information for you from Washington. Do you have a moment?"

Attorney and fellow investigator, Laura de Force Gordon, was standing in the doorway. As per usual, she was wearing her navy-blue dress with high collar and no bustle. Her attitude at all times was one of serious authority, as she saw her duty to citizens to be a woman who could compete with the patriarchy on an equal footing. She knew that Laura, like herself, had been deserted by her philandering husband and left to support herself. Unlike her, Laura had no children, and she held a rather vague distrust of the young.

"Yes, come in. I was just going over what Miriam Levine sent me. We have our work ahead of us, and I am fortunate to have you with me." She sat down on her bed and patted the goose-down mattress. "Sit here."

Laura walked to the bed, glanced over at David Milton, who was still packing her many dresses into the standing trunk, and sat down.

"I trust you have enough fine regalia to impress the fashionable leaders in our nation's capital? If not, you can always start a small dress store on Pennsylvania Avenue."

Laura's dark brown eyes gleamed, as she smiled under the glimmering chandeliered gas lamps of the mansion's bedroom.

Clara's hair was reddish-brown and long, as she sat in her pink dressing gown. Laura's hair was short, black and curly, with graying streaks on the sides. Clara was also a bit chubby, having given birth to five children, and her friend still had the trim waist of a childless, yet middle-aged woman of forty-nine. Clara was thirty-eight, and she began having children as a farm wife, at age fifteen, in Iowa. She was also three inches taller, at five feet and seven inches.

"Please. Tell me what you have. I also have some news."

She grasped her friend's hands in her own.

"I know how you believe we women must use our powers of communication to overcome the masculine power structure. I have the perfect remedy. As you know, our Suffrage Movement was given a brief hearing in Congress, as the Senate recently debated national voting rights for women."

"Indeed. I believe the so-called disputation lasted only two days, on December 8, 1886 and January 23, 1887. I read the transcript in *The Una*. What they argued sounded as if the debate were being held at a local tavern, complete with sawdust on the floors and spittoons for their squirts of chewing tobacco."

They both laughed.

"Yes, the dead Senator, H. B. Anthony, a Whig, was quoted as the distinguished authority on women's rights. Obviously, he couldn't testify in the flesh. Also, our standard bearer, Susan B. Anthony, who is no relation, was not allowed to speak before the main body, nor was any woman, for that matter." She giggled.

"I suppose they needed Adeline Quantrill to channel Senator Anthony's voice," Laura said, referring to Clara's future young daughter-in-law, who was a psychic and could allegedly talk to the spirit world.

"All of the excellent arguments came during the presentation of our group to the Committee of the Judiciary on March 7, 1884. Only five of the official committee members were present that day.

The rest had excuses. Three were supposedly sick in bed, and one had an important meeting concerning the territories." She pointed toward David Milton. "Not in there, Davy. Put my corsets in the small one."

"Yes, and on the day of the final debate before the vote, January 23, 1887, after two-thirds of the House had already approved the amendment to release women from their male bondage, our group outside outnumbered the obviously frightened male senators by the thousands. Also, many of the new states had already passed both voting and educational suffrage during the intervening years. However, not a single one of us was allowed inside those hallowed chambers to confront our detractors."

Laura's voice held its usual loud volume, as she was quite angry.

"But we digress. What information did you bring me?" She leaned forward.

"When the assassination of Judge Marshal Owens took place, I wired Miss Anthony in New York, and we conferred by telegraph about our upcoming criminal trial in Washington D. C. Miss Anthony investigated her membership files, and, lo and behold, Mrs. Mary Ann Shadd Cary, a colored woman and teacher in Washington, knew our client's teacher, Mrs. Mary Terrell, at the Preparatory High School for Negroes. Since they were both members of the National Woman Suffrage Association, they had recruited young Eloise Strong, a former slave, into their group. She is, in fact, a paid member."

"She's a suffragette?"

She squeezed Laura's hands and smiled.

"Yes, she is. Not only that, but Susan B. Anthony, our president, shall be in Washington for the trial, and she's bringing as many members as she can convince, to demonstrate for what they see as a righteous cause against male domination and inhuman capital punishment."

"You mean we shall have our suffragette leaders there?"

She almost squealed with delight at the prospect.

"They see Miss Eloise Strong as a woman who was not only

traumatized by our patriarchal system into sexual degradation, but who was also, because of her mulatto heritage, enslaved in prostitution by those same men who said they fought for human freedom during the Civil War."

Laura reached over to hug her. Clara held her friend at arm's length.

"These men of injustice will not give women the same human dignity they readily gave to Miss Strong's male, formerly enslaved brethren. I say bring on the Attorney General, or President Cleveland himself. We shall not be defeated if we can stand together!"

***

The Preparatory High School for Negroes, 2565 Georgia Avenue, N.W., Washington, D.C. May 4, 1887.

Moses had always seen himself as a type of Renaissance man. He studied architecture, science, religion, and the law, while at Oberlin College in Ohio, and at the University of Michigan, when his parents moved there. Even though his baseball expertise had moved him away from the halls of education, he still maintained a connection with academe wherever he played.

He was the third son of the six children born to Moses W. Walker and Caroline O'Harra Walker, both of whom were of mixed race. His parents had always taught him that education was one of the only ways "we coloreds can become respected by society," and that was why his father had become both a Methodist Episcopal minister and a medical physician. His father could then minister to the white people's souls in their community, and to his own people's bodies in their segregated neighborhood. When "Fleet" decided to play professional baseball and leave his law studies at the university, his father was especially unnerved.

After he began to confront the ignorant prejudice in baseball, he started to visit his parents less frequently. Now, at thirty-one and married, he loved baseball, and yet he didn't want to share the experience with his parents, who were not sports enthusiasts. All they would see would be how hard he had to play, at the most difficult position on the field, and how little he used his mind.

He was out on the diamond speaking to Howard University's baseball team about his experiences as catcher "Fleet Walker," the first Negro to play in the major leagues. A young girl ran up to him from out of the adjoining Miner Building, where the preparatory high school was located. He had spoken there to a group of students just two hours before.

"Mr. Walker! You must come to the auditorium. One of our students, Eloise Strong, has assassinated Judge Marshal Owens!"

The Miner Building was a large, three-story, symmetrically-massed Colonial Revival brick structure; it was prominently situated on a hillside on the east side of Georgia Avenue between Fairmont Street and Howard Place on the Howard University campus. The enrollment was 361, there were nine teachers, exclusive of the instructors in music and drawing, and all nine were now inside the auditorium, whose entrance he was now about to enter.

He remembered the woman the girl said killed Judge Owens because she was much older than the other students, and she was quite attractive. Her teacher, Mrs. Terrell, told him that Eloise had grown-up in Murder Bay, south of Pennsylvania Avenue, near Fifteenth and B Streets. This was where many of the former slaves lived. When she passed her entrance exams, she was able to get a job uptown on Massachusetts, but she still had to commute from where she lived.

Eloise seemed especially interested in what he told the students about his studying law in college. She asked him about social inequality, and he understood her interest.

She was, quite obviously, an attractive woman who could, as his father would phrase it, "pass," if she wanted. In fact, his father, who also looked white, had passed enough to get educated and work in a white community in Ohio, but he had to live with his family in the Negro neighborhood.

Eloise explained that she was not just a mulatto, she was also a slave, and her government identification branded her as such. She told him that women like her were given an extra cross to bear

14

because they could reproduce offspring and were therefore a direct threat to the male power culture of white domination.

As he was also a mulatto, he agreed with her, up to a point. He said that if she was able to make herself valuable to society's future, perhaps as a lawyer, or maybe as an inventor or a scientist, then she would be accepted. That's when the class began to discuss how the white power structure tried to make it seem as if they were all equal, in a variety of ways, right there in Washington.

A male student said he lived in one of the many shacks behind the large houses where the white families lived. He told the class that his row house was on the alley, and his place had no plumbing, and the roof leaked, and there was no concrete beneath the pine wood floor, wherein he and his family of five had to live in two crowded rooms.

"On paper," he said, "it looks like we live right next-door to the whites, but, in reality, we are just like the slaves were on the plantations. My momma even works in the big house, the way the house slaves did!"

It was quite a lively discussion, and he was impressed by the intelligence and critical thinking exhibited by the students. He ended his presentation by telling them that the worst of social inequality was today caused by those in the wealthy classes who made breeding and birthright the most important way to advance, rather than what the Declaration of Independence said it should be: "All men created equal."

As he entered the auditorium, he was immediately approached by Mrs. Mary Terrell, Eloise Strong's teacher. Her face was not as lovely as earlier, as it was now twisted in fear. He imagined she was afraid this type of horrific incident would put the entire school in a poor light. She reminded him of most of the teachers he had been associated with, as her main emphasis was on an optimistic, fearless belief in the goodness of humanity to ultimately do the right thing. To him, the humanity with whom he had come into contact was too controlled by prejudice and fear to make the right choices.

"Mr. Walker, we're so happy you are here! Principal

Cardozo was just about to discuss the way we are going to address this terrible incident."

She motioned for him to sit in one of the folding wood chairs that filled the auditorium. There were only seven chairs occupied at present, and the principal was standing in front of the stage's riser at a rostrum.

Before he sat down, he looked at all the seated teachers as they talked to each other. It reminded him of the white folks in church who used to discuss his father's sermons. Evil seemed to always be out there, waiting for you, unless you kept up your good deeds, your daily prayers, and your understanding of your fellow man. He wondered if these same teachers had much experience out there amongst the ones who wanted you to remain in your place.

"Ladies and gentlemen, please quiet down. This is an emergency, and we must establish our goals and objectives."

He thought the principal looked like a Gingerbread Man with spectacles. This Cardozo was wiping beads of sweat from his brow, looking for an exit, it seemed, and he could picture him shedding his frock coat and undergarments, to make a mad dash out the door to get out of the oven. However, Cardozo finally pulled himself together enough to speak, and his voice had a Scottish lilt that sounded affected. It wasn't the "preaching voice" his father had, but it was close. He was, after all, the principal.

"Miss Eloise Strong has been taken, with utmost care, I might add, to the District Jail. I have been informed that she shall be represented by a legal defense team from the West Coast." He looked down at a sheet of paper on the rostrum. "Clara Shortridge Foltz, Esquire, from San Francisco."

The male teacher next to him spoke.

"Is she a Negro?"

"No, Aaron. She is not. We can have no say in this matter, I am afraid. The Attorney General has appointed the defense counsel, and I was told it was because this legal team can be more objective, as they won't have been subject to all the negative press that is certainly going to be pummeling our school."

Our school? What was this blowhard talking about? What

about the poor woman who could hang by her white neck until she's dead? Didn't these teachers understand how much these whites hated you when you were of mixed-race inheritance? It was as if they believed you purposely planned it that way. This Eloise Strong was going to be seen as a whore and temptress, and her skin color will be seen as her deceitful make-up, created by the Devil himself when her mamma tempted the innocent white man who made her pregnant.

"She was such a strong student. I told her so. She wanted to go to law school."

Mrs. Terrell's husband was speaking. He was the one who was seated in the back of the room when he spoke to the students earlier in the day.

"Be honest, Robert. That girl just wanted to go to Harvard. Howard was too dark for her. This white judge probably told her she was too full of pride to realistically believe she could be accepted."

The same man, Aaron, was again speaking.

Mrs. Terrell stood up to address the others.

"Eloise joined our Negro Suffrage group. She was my best student, and our women told her she could be anything she put her mind to be. Robert was accepted into Harvard. And he graduated, with honors. So, why not another bright student? I don't begrudge her that. Women need to rise up if they have the intelligence and the will to do so!"

Another woman teacher at the end of the row spoke.

"I agree with Mary. We women deserve to be recognized, and why should we always have to go to the Negro schools?"

He had heard enough. He had also gone to those white schools and played with those white boys. But these D. C. "nigrahs" had lived in their little government shelter too long. He stood up, cleared his throat, and raised his hand.

"Yes, brother? Are you that *baseball player*? Mr. Walker?"

Gingerbread Man pointed at him. He made the words "baseball player" sound like a disease of some kind.

"Yes, sir, I am the same. Moses Fleetwood. Has anybody here ever seen a man hanged?"

He looked into each face until each one shook his or her head back at him in the negative.

"I thought not. Well, I have. It was 1881, in August, and I had begun my baseball playing career on a semi-pro team. We were competing in Louisville, Deep South, mind you. It was hotter than Hades, and two of the Eclipse team's players, an all-white team, refused to come out on the field if I was behind the bat. Said they didn't want to smell a 'hot nigger.' The rest of the men on my team decided I needed to sit it out, so I did. But after that game, I was going back to my hotel room at a Negro boarding house when I saw a group of men surrounding a brother in front of the rural town's jail. They had the sheriff in their custody, and they strung up that colored prisoner, if that's what he was, and hanged him right there in front of the law."

He could hear their audible gasps, and it made him feel stronger. When he told his own family this story, they said he needed to pray for the poor man.

"I don't care if this woman has the best defense lawyers on God's green Earth! I don't care if she's Madame Curie herself. If these white devils want her strung up, they will do it. No matter what it takes, and no matter who they have to overpower to do it!"

"I can understand your concern, Mr. Walker, but you should have more faith in our system of justice. This is certainly not Kentucky. Miss Strong is innocent until proven guilty, and if we cooperate with Mrs. Foltz and her team, I believe our student will be given every advantage."

A thin teacher at the end of his row cleaned his spectacles with a handkerchief he extracted from his coat pocket. Moses thought his long nose, frilled white shirt, and narrow eyes made him look like a fop in a play by Shakespeare, as he began to speak.

"The girl was raised in Murder Bay. When those prosecutors start looking into her past, I don't think she stands much of a chance."

He turned to face him. These people needed a lesson in political reality.

"She had to live there because the whites still control the

wealth. If Miss Strong is as intelligent as Mr. and Mrs. Terrell say she is, then we need to support her, to the bitter end, no matter where she had to live."

The fop sat back down, but he had to have the last word. "You don't know this town, Walker. The whites aren't the only ones with color codes."

He moved fast. He stepped around Mary Terrell, grabbed the fop by his frilly collar, and pulled him back up. "I may not know this town, skinny boy, but I know human nature. If we can't stick together, those white demons will exploit the cracks in our resolve faster than you can yell for help."

"Now, gentlemen. No need for physical abuse." Gingerbread weakly struck the rostrum with his fist. "I agree with you, Mr. Walker. However, we shall seek our guidance from professionals. Mrs. Foltz and her retinue will be needing our help, and they will be here in a week on the transcontinental railroad. I suggest we be ready."

***

Later, sipping at a beer at the bar, inside the college tavern on Howard Place, he made a decision to stay and help Eloise Strong any way he could. As he thought about it, this decision had actually been formed during his many days traveling all over the country playing ball. Alone in a boarding house for coloreds, or sitting on the bench during a game, he had resurrected the teachings from his college life and his private readings to formulate his world view.

To him, it was the only answer to the prejudice and anger shown to his people, on a daily basis, from these so-called "freedom-loving" citizens. In his mind, he believed these white devils, even the ones who had been abolitionists during the Civil War, these devils had already made their pact with Mammon. They secretly believed that the Negroes had been responsible for their beloved country tearing itself apart, and that these niggers had to pay for that destruction as long as they lived.

He had no trust in the politics going on around him. Even though baseball was, he believed, a microcosm of the larger society, it was the spiritual union of the African tribal society that needed to be heeded. Even if his people had to form their own towns, cities and even states, right here in the United States, or beyond, it must be done to protect the sacred trust of honesty and self-protection which only a tribe can give.

After the Civil Rights Act of 1875 was rejected by the Supreme Court, in 1883, he had lost all hope in Anglo-Saxon justice, even in its present weak form. For, as he knew, none of the so-called "civil rights" in the South were ever enforced, even during the eight years between the Supreme Court's ruling.

The poor Negro, who had to get a lawyer just to file a grievance for not being allowed to eat at the local cafe, also had no power to become a juror, a landowner, a member of a trade union, or even a member at the local Elks Lodge. But, at least, the law was there until 1883, when it was rejected, 8-1, by the highest court. The way he viewed it, Miss Eloise Strong was probably doing her race a favor by assassinating this newly nominated Supreme Court Justice, Marshal Owens.

He took another big swig from his beer and belched. A few of the students at the tables laughed at him.

His wife, Bella, was now in Trenton, waiting for him to return. He met her when they were children in Mount Pleasant, Jefferson County, Ohio. She later followed him to Michigan after his time at Oberlin College in Ohio. Baseball at Oberlin was limited to interclass play when the college dedicated a new baseball field in 1880. During that inaugural contest, he caught and struck a memorable grand slam. He and his battery mate, Harlan Burket, led the junior class to a win over the senior nine.

Then in 1881, Oberlin College fielded its first varsity intercollegiate team. Members included him, his younger brother Weldy Wilberforce Walker, and Burket. They were all future professional players. The season's final game was a 9-2 win over the University of Michigan. Burket reported to him that he and teammate Arthur Packer so impressed the Michiganders that they were invited to transfer there. They did, in fact, get a scholarship to the University of Michigan, with Weldy joining them in the move. Also accompanying him was then 18-year-old Arabella "Bella"

Taylor.

However, even as a successful player, husband, and father, he met the real truth, behind the scenes in an exhibition game against the Chicago White Stockings, on August 10, 1883. His Toledo Blue Stockings, which would later become a member of the International League and thrust him into the major leagues of 1884, hosted the famous team from Chicago, with its star player, Cap Anson.

With the buzz of the students' conversations going on all around him, he thought about the letter his old Toledo manager, Charlie Morton, had given him as a souvenir of that day. Just like these protected Negro teachers, he had been protected by white Charlie, when Cap Anson said he wouldn't "play with no nigger." Anson did play that day, but later, when the white newspapers covered it, and the people had their way, the team with the first coloreds playing, including him and his brother, Weldy, was driven out of the major leagues. No more civil rights. No more major leagues in 1884.

He took the letter out of his coat pocket, unfolded it, and read it in full once more. He often read it to solidify his belief that there was no justice for the Negro in this land.

Manager Toledo Base Ball Club:

Dear Sir: We the undersigned, do hereby warn you not to put up Walker, the Negro catcher, the evenings that you play in Richmond, as we could mention the names of 75 determined men who have sworn to mob Walker if he comes to the ground in a suit. We hope you will listen to our words of warning, so that there will be no trouble: but if you do not, there certainly will be. We only write this to prevent much blood shed, as you alone can prevent.

Chapter 3: Prosecution

The White House, 1600 Pennsylvania Avenue. West Wing, Oval Office, May 4, 1887.

Stephen Grover Cleveland could see brothels from his office window in the White House. The ladies who worked inside those establishments, he thought, were doing their very best. Lonely bachelors and less than handsome men were able to seek loving and personal comfort from those bosoms and lips.

He had been one of those lonely men just a year before. For two long years, after he was elected President, his sister, Rose, was his social hostess inside the White House. She would much rather spend her time conjugating Greek verbs than she would greeting dignitaries.

But now, Frances, dear Frances, whom he had adored since she was born, was his prized possession, and his betrothed beauty of twenty-one years young. He had been the first President ever to be married inside the White House, the year before. The wedding took place, right next-door, within the Blue Room. His phenomenal rise from Mayor of Buffalo to the presidency had taken only three years, and he viewed Frances as his ultimate reward.

Frank and her mother, Emma, became his financial responsibilities, when Frances was eleven, after his legal partner, Oscar Folsom, died, without a will, in a tragic buggy accident. Frances always called him "Uncle Cleve," and he called her "Frank," the name she was given at birth after her uncle. Now, thanks be to God, she was his popular First Lady, and the public called her Frankie, invigorating the White House with youth, music, and impetuous frivolity.

A country should be run, Grover believed, to allow honest businessmen, farmers, and merchants to accumulate what wealth they needed to become satisfied. Although the people should support the government, the government should not support the people. The people should be permitted to earn as much as they wanted to be free and to pursue their own brand of happiness.

President Cleveland turned back from gazing out the window at the West Wing's version of the cityscape. He had been notified of the assassination of his nominee to the Supreme Court, and good friend, Judge Marshal Owens. His daily calendar of appointments had been, of necessity, thrown off kilter, and this made his stomach growl in protest. His Attorney General, Augie Garland, was taking care of the legal details, and that was a good thing. Garland knew how to think in terms of the collective good. That was Grover's greatest flaw.

As president, Grover knew he was elected because he could see how the individual citizen was being hoodwinked, as he had demonstrated while Governor of New York, taking on the likes of Tammany Hall and John Kelly, but he had very little knowledge about what it would be like if one first considered the best interests of the Family of Man. As a Southern Democrat, after the war, Augie had argued, quite successfully, to get himself reinstated back to practicing law, and then into the Congress of the United States, simply by appealing to the "higher good of humanity," as he called it. That's why Grover had chosen him as his top lawyer. They worked together nicely.

Grover could see himself in the large mirror inside the Oval Office. He recalled the names the press of the opposition had called him during his tenure as the mayor of Buffalo, as Governor of New York, and when he ran for President of the Union. "Big Steve" and "Uncle Jumbo," they'd called him. His Frances enjoyed his 275-pound girth, and she would often whisper in his ear during their lovemaking, "You make me swoon, Uncle Jumbo!" It was their private levity. She never called him that in public.

He hated campaigning, with all that walking around and giving public speeches. The press, he believed, simply swallowed words, mashed them into an unrecognizable pulp with its collective brain, and spewed out one ghastly malapropism and untruth after another. He was holding in his right hand an example of this dastardly reportage.

When his attorney general entered the Oval Office, Grover

addressed him immediately.

"This is a sample of what we'll have to contend against during this trial." Grover held up the article, with the improvised map, and pointed to it. "Hooker's Division, they call it. Which contains 50 saloons and 109 bawdy houses. And, they list 61 places where liquor is sold with a U. S. Government license, but without a city license. Balderdash!"

To the president's dismay, at fifty-five, Augustus Hill Garland was five years his senior, but he looked forty-five. Clean-shaven, baby-faced, with a clear complexion, his pomaded head of full brown hair was like his Secretary of State, Thomas F. Bayard, who was Grover's successor, now that former Vice President, Thomas Hendricks, had died in 1885. Bayard and Garland always contrasted sharply with Grover, who was balding and rotund with walrus mustaches.

Augie also liked to wear the latest European suits, rather than the more conservative business attire with bowed ties preferred by Grover and Thomas. The only consolation to Grover was that Garland was under five feet tall, a very short man.

"You thought those city commissioners were clean, Mr. President. But when the Women's Christian Temperance Union uncovered the fact that Reginald Baldwin owned several saloons in that same Hooker District, we had to replace him from the board. Sometimes, I'm afraid, your faith in men, unencumbered by membership in organizations, does not prove correct, as in this instance."

Grover moved past his desk to stand directly in front of Augustus, again pointing to the article. "Listen to this. 'Grover Cleveland can sit in his bedroom window at the White House and survey this entire territory. He is within sight and gunshot of each of these 109 dens which defy the laws which he is supposed to execute through his commissioners.' Can you believe these lies?"

"I understand, Mr. President, but we need to get back to the matter at hand. I am prosecuting this woman, this former slave and mulatto, for first degree murder. Nobody will be harassing you about where she lived." Garland held up the folder under his arm. "Here, let me read what I have thus far in our case against her."

Grover was still fuming under his breath. "Then, they go on to list the owners of these taverns and bawdy houses, by name and address, mind you . . ."

"Mr. President! You must concentrate. We need to develop a strategy which demonstrates our careful consideration of what's best for the public's safety. The press, as you know, or you *should* know, is now writing about the possible race riots and more assassination attempts that could be made upon other public leaders, even us. There are bigger fish to fry than what you can see out of these White House windows."

"Very well. Let me hear it."

Grover folded his article and tucked it into the inside pocket of his extra-large suit coat.

"My men have isolated the scene at the baseball park. We shall subpoena fifteen people who were eye witnesses, and I am drafting the information today. I will use the witnesses' complaints, along with the tangible evidence we have thus far. Mrs. Foltz has already waived the grand jury process, as is the usual case when there are eye witnesses and the murder weapon is seized."

"Go on. What about the motive? And the mental state of this woman?"

As a former Sherriff of Erie County, Grover had hanged two convicted murderers, so he was very familiar with the process of criminal justice. He knew because this was a woman it would be more difficult to establish the requisite *mens rea*. Juries, especially criminal juries, were often predisposed to believe women acted more irrationally and with little or no deliberation beforehand.

"The negress was attending The Preparatory School for Negroes on the Howard University campus. We discovered in her purse a letter addressed to the Harvard University School of Law. In it, she is petitioning the school for entrance as the first Negro woman to attend. At the bottom of this petition was the typed name of Justice Marshal Owens."

"I see. Therefore, do you believe it would be best to show that letter as the motive behind this woman's dastardly act of murder?"

"As it is I who will be prosecuting, I do think this would be a motive that could be used because of its proximate causal relationship to the knife. When Judge Owens told her he could not sign this letter, for reasons I shall elaborate upon during the trial, she became enraged enough to finally stab him, and hold onto the knife, until the police pried it from his bloody chest. In point of fact, that single letter demonstrates the requisite *mens rea* because it is proof positive she had been thinking about sexually manipulating Owens, for her own purposes, well before today."

Grover liked the way Augie's Southern accent made his words sound slower, more reflective, and smoothly erudite. The attorney general had, in fact, been against slavery, when he was a congressman in Arkansas, just before his state seceded. Only after the war began did Augustus finally become patriotic to the Rebel cause, and it was with grave trepidation that he did so.

"Sexually manipulating? What proof do you have of this?"

"We have witnesses who say this Eloise Strong was Marshal Owens' lover. They saw her going into hotels where they would meet and not come out of a room for days. She certainly must have been after something from him, don't you agree?"

Grover was finally aroused. It made him recall his own sexual manipulation by that alcoholic sales clerk and divorcee, Maria Halpin, in Buffalo, back when he was a young attorney. The wench had become impregnated by one of her many suitors, and she came after him, the only bachelor she knew, in order to seek restitution. Certainly, because he did bed her, he paid her five hundred dollars, but only after she agreed to name the child after his law partner, and father of his Frances, Oscar Folsom. In punishment for her manipulation, Grover had her placed into the Providence Lunatic Asylum and the child into the Buffalo orphanage. When she was released from the asylum, shown to be sane, he continued paying her child support for the tyke in return for no further harassment on her part.

The entire fiasco had almost cost him his presidential election in 1884 against Republican James Blaine. He had won the popular vote by only one-quarter of one percent. Now, with his first term ending, this murder of his Supreme Court nominee might also prove his downfall, unless they could convict the perpetrator under honorable circumstances.

"Yes, I understand. She wanted the government, represented by an Appellate Court Justice, to give her a free pass into Harvard University, the most prestigious college in our great nation. As you know, when I attended Harvard's two hundred fiftieth anniversary, last year, they wanted to bequeath me with an honorary degree. I refused it, as I told the men, because I was not worthy, having never attended any college before."

Garland nodded. "I remember. I was there."

"And now, we have this woman, this sexual Jezebel, who attempts to blackmail an officer of one of this nation's highest courts? Just so she can get into college without earning her way? Augie, you know, you can also show this manipulation as a lesson to those who would use their fair sex as a devious method of acquiring wealth and fame. Women like these suffragettes, who attempt to blackmail our nation into giving them voting rights, just so they can leave the home and family, which should, in fact, be their first duty!"

"She is also one of those." Garland said.

"One of what?"

Grover paused and twisted his mustache.

"A suffragette."

Grover clapped his hands.

"Aha! There, you see? Fate has its own mastery over all our human designs, does it not? We can kill the proverbial two birds with one gigantic stone of capital punishment."

"Two birds? What are those?"

Grover smiled at the baby-faced innocence of his attorney general.

"The black bird, which is a vengeful murderess, and the red bird, which is the socialist suffrage movement."

"I see. I will keep that in mind. That is the main reason I chose our opponent, Clara Shortridge Foltz. She is a known suffragist of the highest order. No doubt, her obvious bias will get her into deep trouble during the trial, as it has in the past."

Grover wrapped his arm around his shorter friend's shoulders and guided him to the door.

"Augie, we can finish this at Old Ebbitt Grill. I'm in the mood for oysters and stout, how about you? And, when we finish, I shall be ready to meet my young bride at our rendezvous away from this White House of political ill repute."

Augie followed his boss out the door, where they were met by two of the guards appointed to follow Grover wherever he went. There had been letters from deranged sorts who had threatened the president's life for what they termed "robbing the cradle."

Grover hollered down the hall toward the open door of his personal secretary.

"Colonel Lamont! We are now leaving!"

Augie ran up to him as he rushed through the door held open by one of the guards.

"Are you enjoying the little retreat you've built away from the White House to protect you both from the press?"

"She loves it, even though all the promoters have been placing her lovely visage in advertisements, for everything, from perfume and candy to corsets."

They both laughed.

"I understand she is also speaking out against suffrage. What is her main argument?"

Grover chuckled again.

"She has informed the press and me that she believes women have not yet been educated sufficiently to take on that serious responsibility. Coming from a graduate of Wells College, that is indeed saying something, is it not? She's fluent in Latin, German and French. She is also, as you know, a wonderful pianist."

"Yes, she is. I shall also use the fact that she supports the Home for Friendless Colored Girls. Our defendant, as a matter of fact, should have resided there, instead of living in Murder Bay."

Garland spat into the gutter next to the black presidential carriage.

Grover turned to confront his attorney general.

"She does not officially support that charity! I told her specifically to stay away from that home until we were assured re-election for a second term."

"But there have been reports that she was seen at the home just recently, after having escorted two colored girls there, whom she discovered eating from garbage cans in an alley."

"I will put an end to that! I had to let go of Frederick Douglass from his job as Recorder of Deeds, after he married that white woman. I cannot have Negro miscegenation ruin my chances in the South for re-election. You know that, Augie."

"But, Mr. President. You now have no colored person in your administration, and during this trial, I shall have to confront the press concerning the treatment of Negroes after the Supreme Court's recent ruling against the Civil Rights Act of 1875. It will not look good for us at all."

"Balderdash! My re-election will hinge upon my ability to go with the times. And the times are moving away from the freeloading handouts of the Reconstruction Era and into the Cleveland era of self-sufficiency."

Grover stomped up to the waiting carriage, making a mental note to again speak with Frances about her activities. Her recent attendance at a meeting of the Women's Christian Temperance Union had already caused a big argument between them. She had finally agreed not to ban alcohol from being served at their White House dinners, even though she had personally taken the vow of abstinence from partaking of the "devil's spirit," as she had called alcohol.

The spring night air was filled with the songs of birds, and just over the fence, near the guard shack, Grover could see and hear the distant ruckus of Pennsylvania Avenue, with its bawdy houses and taverns. More closely, however, were the members of the press, their squirming bodies pushed against the wire fence like trapped sparrows, shouting at him and flashing their cameras.

He inhaled deeply and climbed, with some effort, into his private carriage. He noticed the full moon, a portent of insane behavior, and he was eager to experience all the other sensory delights that awaited him that evening.

Grover was happy to later go home to their love nest at Red Top, the twenty-seven-acre working farm, in the Georgetown Heights section of Washington. Frankie would be waiting there, her raven, flowing black hair still moist from her bath, her alabaster hands poised above the piano keys, and her deeply passionate, heaven-blue eyes drawing him closely within her web of adoring love.

***

Home for Friendless Colored Girls, Erie Street, Meridian Hill, N.W., Washington, D. C., May 4, 1887.

The First Lady of the United States, "Frankie," as the press called her, was seated in a rocking chair, reading from an old copy of *Uncle Tom's Cabin*. Five colored girls, ranging in age from five to fourteen years, were seated around her on the carpeted floor.

Beside Frances, Mrs. Caroline Taylor was settled in a stuffed chair next to the brick fireplace. She glanced over at her friend between passages. Caroline was smiling, her dark face aglow, staring into the roaring warmth of the evening's blaze. Mrs. Taylor was the founder and President of the Women's Christian Union, which served as the Board of Directors for the home.

You ought to be ashamed, John! Poor, homeless, houseless creatures! It's a shameful, wicked, abominable law, and I'll break it, for one, the first time I get a chance; and I hope I shall have a chance, I do! Things have got to a pretty pass, if a woman can't give a warm supper and a bed to poor, starving creatures, just because they are slaves, and have been abused and oppressed all their lives, poor things!

She saw that her words were mesmerizing the five pieces of chocolate in corduroy skirts and matching blouses. The House's insignia of a little colored girl, standing alone in the center of a town, was stitched upon their pockets. All five of them stared up at her in various states of physical repose.

As she reached a break in the reading, Mrs. Taylor stood up, and Frances, taking the cue, also arose. She had great respect for her colored friend, whom she had met at a meeting of the Women's Christian Union, shortly after Frances had moved into the White House for the social season.

Caroline informed the First Lady that she had two projects to help homeless Negro girls who were found wandering the streets. One was the Home in which they were now visiting, and the other was a Christmas charity that provided food and gifts to many disadvantaged coloreds in the Washington D. C. slums.

"Time for bed, girls! Pastor James will be here tomorrow morning for your Bible lesson." Caroline motioned to the Negro housekeeper. "Be certain Emily brushes her teeth, Mrs. Sanders. I shall be in later to supervise your prayers."

One by one, each of the girls came up to Frances and gave her a hug and a kiss on her cheek. "Thank you, Mrs. Cleveland," they each said, with downcast eyes.

"Keep up your studies, girls. The future will be bright if you learn all you can and stay on the straight and narrow."

She inhaled deeply with satisfaction. After the children were taken upstairs, she turned to her friend, who had returned to her chair near the fireplace.

"Before you go up, Caroline. May I speak with you about a personal matter?"

She leaned forward, brushing the hair at the back of her neck with her right hand.

Her hairstyle, with the strands at the bottom cut in a circle, had become quite popular with women all over the country. So had her low-cut necklines, which exposed her white shoulders. Even though the Women's Christian Temperance Union had formally complained that the style would "corrupt young women and tempt men's unwholesome thoughts," Frances had ignored their admonishments and continued wearing her casual dresses that way.

"I came over here after Mr. Henry Watterson, the former congressman and journalist, visited me at Oak View this morning. There has been a horrible tragedy. A young mulatto woman named

Eloise Strong has been arrested for the assassination of Justice Marshal Owens."

When she saw her friend's eyes widen, she knew Caroline had not heard about this news.

"May Jesus preserve us! We shall all be blamed!"

Caroline, Frances realized, was well aware of the current politics, which were moving away from civil rights for the Negro and into a more conservative era of self-sufficiency, bigotry, and parsimony.

"That is my concern. My husband told me he appointed Mr. Owens because he would support my husband's anti-tariff policies and his philosophy of no more hand-outs for the coloreds. I want you to help me assist this woman. However, the President cannot know I am doing it. Do you understand?"

She took the dark hands of Caroline Taylor into her own. She once more appreciated the contrast in their coloring. After accepting Cleve's proposal, he wanted her to travel to Europe to learn its customs, so she could be a good hostess in the White House. During her voyage to Europe, after graduation and alone, she had seen that, unlike in the United States, the color differences were not noticed. Especially in France, where young white men could be seen strolling, hand-in-hand, with Negro women, along the Avenue des Champs-Élysées. She had first appreciated that contrast then, and when she saw the beautiful children born from such romance, she made a silent vow to help bring the two races together for the betterment of civilization everywhere.

"I will do what I can, Frances. I would expect our religious community to come together for our own protection. Do you know the history of this young woman?"

"Mr. Watterson says she was a student at the Preparatory High School at Howard University. She grew-up in Murder Bay, but she excelled in her studies. What's important is that she was born an out-of-wedlock slave in Virginia."

She released Caroline's hands and studied her friend's expression. Caroline looked tentative.

"A slave and mulatto. A double curse." Caroline frowned.

"What do you think you can do to assist her in her hour of need?"

"Attorney General Garland will be prosecuting her. That means, according to political protocol, my husband is prosecuting her. When the time is proper, I want to show the public that I am against Capital Punishment. I believe that Miss Strong will be prosecuted to punish all Negroes, but especially female Negroes who overstep their expected position in life."

She had not thought out her position very carefully. She never expressed her thoughts to Mr. Watterson. She wanted to keep her plans a secret between her fellow Christian women—especially the Negro women—and herself.

"What exactly do you want from us, Frances? I have no authority to promise anything until I've met with my peers. I'm certain you must be aware of that."

There was a knock on the door. It was Jasper Woodley, her Negro chauffer. Standing beside him was Grover Cleveland's personal secretary, Colonel Daniel S. Lamont.

She would know that balding head and brush mustache anywhere. The old white gentleman was not a military officer. He was given the honorary title as a political prompter for Grover Cleveland during his years as New York governor. She and the colonel had a silent agreement about her private activities. Whenever he knew about her husband's whereabouts, he would keep her apprised, so she could stay out of trouble.

She ran up to Colonel Lamont and took his arm.

"What is it, Danny? Is my husband safe?"

She had reverted to her youthful fearfulness. Hers was the fear of being an only child and having to see her only sister, Nellie, die in infancy, and her father die in a buggy accident. Grover Cleveland was her rock, her strong benefactor and protector, but he was also, ironically, a challenge to her female independence. This produced a mixture of extreme joy and anxiety in her youthful psyche.

"The President is out with Augustus, but he expects you back at home. I suggest that you get back there promptly."

She nodded, and she exhaled in relief. She turned toward

Mrs. Taylor, remembering her earlier question.

"I need you to keep me informed, Caroline. I want to visit her as soon as possible."

She kept her gaze upon her friend as she backed out of the front door of the small cottage on the hill. When Caroline nodded, she turned and followed both men to her awaiting carriage. She saw that the moon in the sky was full, and she whispered a saying her mother taught her as a child, when she was afraid of the dark.

"We are born to kiss the stars and dance with the Moon."

She twirled around, doing a fancy two-step, as she grabbed onto Jasper's strong hands, and he lifted her up into the carriage.

Chapter 4: Visitors

Women's section of the D. C. Central Detention Facility, 1901 D Street, Southeast, Washington D. C., May 5-12, 1887.

Detective Sergeant Hubert Abercrombie knew that Officer Erin Scully was Irish Catholic and that she believed she was chosen to be Eloise Strong's matron at the D. C. Jail because they had the same initials. ES. Also, like the prisoner, Scully was a bastard orphan child. She learned to be a transcriber of short hand and a typist through the Irish charities, just as Eloise had learned through the Negro charities.

To make matters more coincidental, Officer Scully was born the same year, 1863, as Miss Strong, and she was what was called a "black Irish," which meant she had kinky black hair and dark-brown eyes. According to Miss Scully, this was supposedly caused by the African Moorish pirates' occupation of West Cork, Ireland in the Middle Ages.

Abercrombie had, at first, been amused by how well the officer and the prisoner had got on together. They seemed to have a special, almost mysterious affinity, and this was what bothered him the most when Scully never appeared for work on Thursday.

Scully's job was to allow only one visitor, who had made a special appointment beforehand, per day. She was also to take down all that was said and to transcribe it for the jail's record. Finally, each visitor could only stay five minutes inside the visitor's room of the women's section of the jail.

Officer Scully had kept a written record, each of the seven days, and every visitor was allowed to bring a gift for the prisoner. Scully also kept a record of the gifts. She did not have to describe the visitor or write down his or her personal information other than the full name.

When Miss Scully never appeared for work, Detective Abercrombie drove, by government buggy, out to Scully's residence at 218 Fifteenth Street, Murder Bay, where he discovered that Scully had, against regulation, brought the bottle of brandy, one of the visitor's gifts, to her apartment. The empty bottle was the first object he saw on a small nightstand at the side of her bed in the one-room flat. She had also brought home the hand-written transcriptions.

He found the dead body of Erin Scully, at 10:20 in the morning, on Thursday, May 12, 1887. She was fully clothed, lying on the bare wood floor, at the foot of her single bed. She was wearing a red nightdress. Her body was positioned with the right side of her face on the floor, her head looking toward the transcribed documents, which were about six inches away. Her left leg was raised slightly, and her right leg was straight. She was barefoot. Both of her arms encircled the documents as if she were protecting them. He could see no apparent abrasions or wounds on her body.

Erin Scully had not reported for work on the same day the prisoner's attorney, Clara Shortridge Foltz, was to visit her client back at the jail.

He bent down, picked up the transcription, and read the following contents:

May 5, Frederick Douglass

Gift: Angel's Trumpet flowers inside a pot, with soil.

Dialogue: FD and ES

FD: *These are for you, Miss Strong. When I read about your arrest, I wanted to be the first to tell you that I empathize with your plight. Have they treated you well?*

ES: *I am very honored, Mr. Douglass. Yes, I have been treated well. Everybody's been polite to me, and I am fed regularly, with changes of clothing, and my own toilet. No bathing, as yet, but I would assume that will be allowed when security is approved.*

FD: *I wanted you to know that I am in contact with every Negro civil rights group and women's group in the country. They shall know that you were cut from the same slave cloth as I, and I will support your right to a fair and impartial trial.*

ES: *I have no doubts. My story needs to be told. I am a*

student of the Constitution, as I know you are. Negro women have been deprived of most of the rights guaranteed therein. Thomas Jefferson, a man who impregnated his slave and freed others, understood that when the rights of human beings are being suppressed by the government, then that government must be overthrown. In my mind, my act was to overthrow an officer of that government who was suppressing my rights.

FD: *I sympathize with your argument, dear lady, but you did not act within the present laws of the land. Others will argue that you are keeping the suffrage of women—especially Negro women— suppressed because you ignored the law. Your act, they will say, was selfish and indignant.*

ES: *I do not wish to discuss the specifics of my case, as I am well aware of the criminal statutes concerning attorney and client privileges. I just want you to know that when my complete story comes out, the people will know that I acted in the best interests of all women and all those whose rights have been ignored since the first slave was brought to this country. I am certain you can understand that, Mr. Douglass.*

FD: *I do understand. Our brethren have risen up in the past against such oppression. Nat Turner and many others were punished, as you are being punished, and I was also beaten and have fought injustice all my many years. But you are now at the mercy of the justice system that has appointed a white woman as your counsel, and you will be judged by white men. You need to be vigilant as to what this really means. That was all I wanted to convey. Good day to you, miss, and may God have mercy upon your soul.*

May 6, Augustus Garland

Gift: box of tea bags

Dialogue: AG and ES

AG: *I know the rotgut coffee they serve here, so I brought you this tea. I simply wanted to inform you that your counsel, headed by Mrs. Clara Shortridge Foltz, Esquire, will be here to meet you on Thursday. You shall be given every consideration as to the discovery evidence being brought to trial against you, and your time with your attorneys will be made private and secure.*

ES: *I have nothing to say to you or to any member of your administration. I believe the Fifth Amendment covers my right to this.*

AG: *In point of fact, when the courts have obtained evidence legally against the accused, a person may not use the Fifth Amendment to protect herself from the court. I am afraid you are not allowed to have a grand jury because it has been waived due to the circumstances of having the eyewitnesses who saw you holding the murder weapon when it was plunged into the heart of Justice Owens.*

ES: *I will meet with my attorney. In point of fact, you do not have the right to say who is or who is not a guilty person, under the Creator's law. Only God does. As I am a child of God, then my personhood is not in question.*

AG: *Our courts, I am sad to report, have not, as yet, reached such angelic standards. We shall soon meet in such a courtroom on Earth, Miss Strong. Good day to you.*

May 7, Moses Walker

Gift: perfume

Dialogue: MW and ES

MW: *I do not wish you to be insulted by my gift. As I have been a guest of such accommodations before, I know the odors are never the most pleasant. I believe the French began the use of perfume in the Middle Ages, before they perfected the science of an adequate sewer system.*

ES: *Mr. Walker, what a pleasure to see you again. I apologize. The circumstances make this very uncomfortable.*

MW: *I simply wanted to say that if you become endangered while incarcerated, or while being transported to or from the court, I will be watching closely to protect you. The person or persons who harm you shall be noted. And you will be avenged.*

ES: *Although that is quite chivalrous of you, I don't believe I shall be in any danger. The attorney general has assured me that my safety will be his utmost concern. Perhaps you could protect me from the press? Their invective, it would seem, could cause much more damage to my chances in court.*

MW: *I believe you are aware that the United Kingdom's judicial system prevents any such trial by the press. They, in fact, prevent coverage in the newspapers, and contempt by publication is a criminal offense by common law. Sadly, in our system, you are already being convicted in the press, but there is nothing I, nor anybody else, can do. I have also been a victim of the press, although my activities were during games of baseball.*

ES: *I admire your gallantry nonetheless. I also appreciate your offer of protection. Your wife and child, I am certain, are in good hands.*

MW: *Please, Miss Strong. Tell me this. Why did you kill him?*

ES: *I discovered, perhaps too late, that I was again a slave.*

MW: *A slave? How can that be? The Emancipation Proclamation has given us our freedom for many years now.*

ES: *I will not discuss it. I have said too much. Please, do not risk your life on account of me. I am doomed. If I should die, you can find the answer at Meridian Hill.*

May 8, Sarah Bernhardt

Gift: Book on Witchcraft

Dialogue: SB and ES

SB: *Oh, my dear woman! I come to you as Ophelia. The insanity of the late hour makes my visit, like hers was in front of*

Hamlet, a mad gesture of female futility. I know your greatness was not fulfilled, and I wish only that you use your magical reality and conviction to cast a spell over these proceedings and escape the demonic clutches of the gallows!

ES: *To be in your presence is magic enough, Divine Sarah. Why have you come to see an unfortunate like me? I am in my last throes of pain and humiliation.*

SB: *I am on my Farewell Tour around the world. I read about your arrest and your background. It is very similar to my own. I was not a slave to a master who owned me, but I was a Jew who needed to use the aristocracy to neutralize the prejudice against me. My mother overcame her poverty by becoming a courtesan, as you have done. I learned acting because the rich gave me a chance to do so. You were not allowed to go to law school because of this one rich man who condemned you. Is this not true?*

ES: *I suppose I could have attended Howard University's School of Law. But I knew my own teacher, Mr. Robert Terrell, was a Negro man who graduated from Harvard's law school, with honors, and yet no law firm in Washington ever gave him a position. That is how he became a teacher. I wanted to break the barrier of prejudice because of color, and I thought I could do it. I am white, like they are. And yet, as I now understand, their prejudice is much deeper than mere skin color. It comes from what Mr. Moses Walker calls birthright privilege. They believe they are better because of their nobility of birth.*

SB: *Your matron has told me I must leave. I shall be following your case, and I am going to use my influence to bring your struggle to light. When I was your age, I used to prepare for acting in tragedies by sleeping in a coffin. This cell is your coffin, but your treatment in this country is what is tragic. Abiento, mademoiselle.*

May 9, Henry Watterson

Gift: honey and apples

Dialogue: HW and ES

HW: *Hello, Miss Strong. I am the Editor-in-Chief of the Louisville Courier-Journal. I was also a congressman for two years. I have never been a believer in slavery, although I did serve in the South's cause during the War of Sections. I have come today to warn you of a threat about which you and your people may not be aware.*

ES: *I must admit. I have not heard that express term used for the Civil War since I was in Virginia. My master used it. As for your belief or non-belief in the economics of slavery, I cannot abide either if you chose to fight on the Confederate side. In my mind, the South fought to keep their traditions, and their wealth and standard of living could not have been kept without the practice of slavery. As for your warning, what could be worse than the loss of civil rights and the continuing repression of women?*

HW: *I certainly respect your intelligence, and I am not against the suffrage of women, as you seem to imply. As you are a student of history, then perhaps you know about the incident of the bloody shirt? As with most tales about politicians, it is fraught with myth.*

ES: *I believe it was a reference to a speech made by Republican Congressman and former Union General, Benjamin Butler, of Massachusetts. He was condemning the torture of a Republican working in the South during Reconstruction. It was the Ku Klux Klan that committed the felonious assault, and Mr. Butler's detractors said that while he spoke on the House floor, he waived the bloody shirt of that man who had been beaten.*

HW: *Quite right. However, the Massachusetts congressman never waved any shirt at all. The speech simply made a rhetorical reference to the shirt, but there was no tangible shirt used during the speech. What I am attempting to explain, in a less than editorial brevity, is that one of the groups, the Redshirts, that sprang from that misunderstood invective from a cartoon in Puck Magazine, has made a direct threat on the lives of anyone who demonstrates in Washington on your behalf.*

ES: *I have no knowledge of such a group. Who are they, and what do they represent?*

HW: *They are a militia group that proudly wears red whenever they demonstrate against carpetbaggers from the North. They have blocked Republican voters and Negro freedmen voters through paramilitary violence. I want you to tell your people to be wary of anybody in the crowd who wears red, as this is their flag of bravery against what they see as the pollution of the white race. I will be authoring an editorial against such threats and acts of violence, but the warning I wanted to give you needed to be personal. I am a friend of the First Lady, Frances Cleveland, as we enjoy the same music. Her Christian group is going to be speaking out against this Southern plague, and she told me she would be visiting you as well. I am against Capital Punishment, and I will be writing about that in an editorial on your behalf. Good day, Miss Strong.*

May 10, Frances Cleveland

Gift: Pisco brandy

Dialogue: FC and ES

FC: *I don't consume alcoholic beverages, but I have brought this Peruvian liquor for you, as I believe you need some kind of spiritual respite from what you've been suffering. I spoke with the Attorney General, and he gave me permission. I want you to know that I will work to make certain you are treated with respect and Christian dignity, Miss Strong.*

ES: *Dignity is all I have left, I am afraid, Mrs. Cleveland. When Joan of Arc was set on fire, for going against the code of proper female behavior in the Middle Ages, I don't imagine she was worried about what impression she was making on future women warriors. Her success, if there was any, was that she was able to defeat the enemy. In my mind, the enemy was represented by Mr. Owens. I don't suppose you can understand that, can you?*

FC: *I understand that you are intelligent, independent and strong, as your surname would imply. However, your fear of the power structure in our country led you down a perilous road. My good friend, Mrs. Caroline Taylor, for example, came from a similar background as you, but she chose a much more judicious, if you will, method of assisting the female cause. If you had simply reached out to her, instead of going all alone, then the resultant tragedy may have been prevented. Can you understand that?*

ES: *My mother was a good Christian woman and a slave. She was owned by a white man, as were we all. And, when I realized that so-called free women were also owned by white men, I became a female warrior. The enemy is within these United States, and I am now victorious, for the moment, until the American press burns me at the stake for betraying the feminine mystique of my gender. But, the noose, I believe, represents the realistic punishment by the men who now condemn civil rights for the Negro. I will burn at the stake of public opinion, but I'll die from the rope of lynching minds, like Judge Owens, who prevent equality between the races.*

FC: *Those are gallant words. I simply want you to see what you could have been, had your self will and stubbornness not overcome your good sense. I have asked Mrs. Taylor to visit you tomorrow, and she will explain what might have been your saving grace. May God have mercy on your soul.*

ES: *Strange you should say that. One of my intellectual betters, Frederick Douglass, also bid me farewell with the same spiritual mercy. I much rather prefer the abiento from an actress. I know you speak fluent French, so the meaning should not escape you. As the gladiators of old used to say, before they fought to their deaths, inside the Roman Coliseum, for the entertainment of the masses, we who are about to die, salute you!*

May 11, Caroline Taylor

Gift: corn bread

Dialogue: CT and ES

CT: *Then I heard a voice from heaven say, write this: Blessed are the dead who die in the Lord from now on.*

ES: *Yes, says the Spirit, they will rest from their labor, for their deeds will follow them.*

CT: *Jesus said to her, I am the resurrection and the life. The one who believes in me will live, even though they die. And whoever lives by believing in me will never die. Do you believe this?*

ES: *So will it be with the resurrection of the dead. The body that is sown is perishable, it is raised imperishable. It is sown in dishonor; it is raised in glory. It is sown in weakness; it is raised in power. If there is a natural body, there is also a spiritual body.*

CT: *So we fix our eyes not on what is seen, but on what is unseen, since what is seen is temporary, but what is unseen is eternal.*

ES: *He will wipe every tear from their eyes. There will be no more death, or mourning, or crying, or pain, for the old order of things has passed away.*

Abercrombie folded the transcribed documents and tucked them into his frock coat pocket. Before leaving for the jail downtown, he took out the tape he brought, for just such a purpose, and he strung it throughout the small apartment, especially surrounding the area where Miss Scully's body was lying.

Downstairs, he knocked on the landlord's apartment door and told him to lock Apartment 4. He explained that it was now a crime scene, and that if anyone entered the area, he or she would be arrested by police. The detective also explained that there would be uniformed policemen dispatched to the location as soon as he returned to the D. C. Jail.

About one-half hour later, when Abercrombie arrived back at the jail, the sidewalk beside the entrance on D Street was filled with news reporters and camera men. They were huddled before seven officers, who were holding them back with truncheons.

Abercrombie pushed through the crowd, nodding to the officers, and when he passed through the main entrance, an attractive woman, wearing an orange dress and a matching straw hat, was talking to the uniformed desk sergeant. The sergeant, seeing him, pointed in his direction. The woman rushed toward him.

"Detective Abercrombie? I am Clara Foltz, Miss Strong's attorney. I don't know where to begin."

Her hazel eyes were glistening with emotion, and when she yanked him by his right arm, he could feel her hand shaking. She guided him back to the cell where her client was incarcerated.

Several uniformed officers followed them, whispering among themselves. Abercrombie knew there was something afoot, and when he saw the body of the young woman on the floor, next to the cot, he understood.

Chapter 5: Mystery

Women's section of the D. C. Central Detention Facility, 1901 D Street, Southeast, Washington D. C., May 12, 1887.

Clara had experienced many reversals of fortune in her life. In fact, she would have to categorize them into personal and professional experiences. Personally, she once believed she could be a happy mother and teacher, married to a proud Union veteran of the Civil War. Reversal. She now was an over-worked civil servant, lawyer, and part-time mother, and her husband was married to a much younger woman in San Jose, both living happily on his government pension.

Professionally, if not for the generous largesse of Mrs. Mary Hopkins, the heiress to the Hopkins' railroad fortune, she would be without a home for her parents, her best friend, and her five children. Reversal. She had lost all three of her court cases, and today, she discovered that her most important opportunity to show her attorney skills had been struck down, like the national suffrage vote for women. She now had to wire the demented Mrs. Hopkins for the money to get back home.

She now had no employment as a defense attorney paid by the U. S. Government. In addition, she was faced with the enigmatic murder of her client, Eloise Strong, and the ultimate task of communicating with her client's former jailer, Detective Sergeant Abercrombie, who was standing in front of her.

She learned the skills of detection from Captain Isaiah Lees in San Francisco. In the flash of a tragic moment, she was now dependent upon the expertise of this little man in an oversized blue suit and vest, standing a head shorter, and apologizing profusely to her about what had happened to her client inside his jail.

His eloquent speech was incongruous with his horribly scarified face, bald head, and missing eyebrows above his close-set, honey-colored eyes.

"I see you are staring. My officers call me Elephant Man behind my back. I am afraid I have scar tissue all over my body, and

46

my hair and brows never grew back. Such are the hazards of going inside burning shacks to rescue row house alley Negroes. The city's firemen didn't believe it was worth the risk, I suppose. Although, several apologized to me, after they saw the damage. I am afraid I now look fifteen years older than my forty-five."

"I'm terribly sorry, Detective. For your personal injuries, and for the loss of my client. Do you know if there is a connection between the death of Officer Scully and Miss Strong?"

She wanted to get to the heart of the matter, even if she were powerless to do anything about it.

Abercrombie took out a collection of papers from the inside pocket of his coat.

"I have this transcript kept by my jail matron. I discovered it, near her dead body, on the floor of her apartment in Murder Bay."

"A transcript? A suicide note?"

She reached out to take the papers, but he pulled his gloved hand back.

"I can't let you read it yet. No. It's a legal transcript kept by Officer Scully. There were seven visitors who came to the jail to talk with your client. This is a record of every word they said." He tucked the sheets back inside his coat pocket. "What worries me is that Scully took the transcript home, along with one of the gifts given to Miss Strong. A bottle of Peruvian brandy."

"Which visitor brought this gift? Did Eloise drink any of it? Are you checking for poisons?"

Her mind was flashing like an inquisitive lightning storm.

"Slow down, Mrs. Foltz. I just returned from her apartment. I must send out the Forensics and Crime Scene officers. How much do you know about your client?" Abercrombie began to walk away from the desk sergeant. "Will you join me? It's not proper to discuss a case here."

Was he asking her to join him as a fellow investigator? It might be possible, if she could convince Mrs. Hopkins to foot the bill.

As they walked away from the main desk, a uniformed officer rushed up to Abercrombie and handed him a message. The detective read it, and he eventually escorted her into a small room next to the long passageway leading toward the prison cells beyond.

Once inside the detective's office, they sat across from each other. She was thinking about the research she had done concerning her new client. Ah Toy and Trella Evelyn had done most of it, and then they wired it to her on the train, as it sped toward Washington D. C. from San Francisco.

"I shall be honest with you, Mrs. Foltz. I have just been informed by the attorney general that the White House will no longer be in charge of this case. I have been appointed as the lone investigator into what happened."

She was astounded.

"How can that be? My client has been murdered under the jurisdiction of the President himself. The world will know about this, I can assure you."

Abercrombie lowered his head. He let out a breath of air and then raised back up to stare at her once again.

"You don't know much about this town, do you?"

"No, I suppose I don't. Can you explain? I am aware of corruption, however, and I would wager this might be your response."

The detective smiled for the first time, but it was a slightly crooked grin.

"President Cleveland, when he first entered office, in 1886, in order to refute President Arthur's policy, sent in eighteen companies of federal troops to prevent the ravaging of Indians and theft of their land, in the Dakota Territories, by greedy settlers. These were the same Sioux Nations who had been marched across the country from their former homes, many of them dying along the way."

"Yes, I remember that. My friend, Dr. McFarland, who was going to examine Miss Strong, is also a student of the Native tribes. He called their march the Trail of Tears."

"Indeed. However, after the election voting was over, President Cleveland, this year, signed the Dawes Act, which partitioned all Indian land into small parcels owned by individuals in the tribe. It was a way to steal land by buying it from individuals who would give up their native culture and religion in exchange for U. S. citizenship and some money."

"I see. The government was allowed to divide and conquer what little was still owned by the collective tribes. No need for troops to be deployed in order to get the land. In addition, the tribal members would become good Christian citizens, so the public would be pleased. *Ingenious*."

"Quite. Now, I suppose you can understand why President Cleveland won't pursue this case. Your client, as long as she was not alone, was somebody to be reckoned with, like the tribal leaders of the Sioux Nation during the election. Now that she is dead, she is no longer a group threat. She will soon be forgotten. As a result, I am the lone cavalry officer who is appointed to work for the Negro tribe, so to speak."

She laughed.

"I like you, Mr. Abercrombie. Better than that. I believe you. I also may be able to get financial backing to assist you in your search for the murderer of these two women."

She reached out and took his two scarred hands into hers.

"I was rather hoping you would say that. My budget for this endeavor has also been substantially reduced."

She noticed his smile, this time, and it was quite authentic.

"I am able to offer you some other expertise. Dr. Andrew McFarland is an excellent toxicologist who is familiar with a wide range of drugs and poisons. He studied in Paris under Mateu Orfila."

"Yes, we use Orfila's text in our department. An excellent resource. Dr. McFarland would be welcomed."

"Two other members on my defense counsel team may be able to assist, but I have also brought my young son along. I was hoping they could take care of him while we were not in court. Attorney Laura Gordon and Captain of Detectives Isaiah Lees are their names."

"I don't believe we shall need their assistance as yet. In fact, I would like us to first go to the laboratory. Could you ring up Dr. McFarland? Is he staying at a local hotel? Most of our large hotels now have telephones."

"Yes. I can do that. Dr. McFarland would be eager to assist us. Do you suspect poison as the murder weapon?"

She leaned forward, eager to hear his response.

"I really can't say as yet. I never answered your earlier question about who brought Eloise Strong the gift of Peruvian brandy because I didn't want anybody to overhear what I said. First Lady Frances Cleveland brought that gift."

"My goodness! But you said the bottle was empty. If the liquor contained poison, then we would need to work with the coroner to get a sample from the bodies."

"I don't know yet. My crime scene officers will bring the bottle back, and there may be some residual liquid remaining. We shall see. The cause of death must first be determined, and I would like your Dr. McFarland to be there when the coroner determines it. Obviously, it won't be determined until both bodies are taken to the morgue."

"Obviously. However, we had a recent experience with what we thought were, at first, obvious circumstances."

Abercrombie smiled.

"Oh yes? Please tell me more."

"There was poisoning of patients being experimented upon by the superintendent and the scientist, Francis Galton, at the Stockton State Insane Asylum. Dr. McFarland analyzed the poison's ingredients, and he determined it was a mixture of opiates and the hallucinogen, peyote, in liquid form. But, later, we also discovered that the doctors in the asylum were giving all the mental patients the peyote in injections. One of the patients, a twelve-year-old girl, was switching the murder weapons with poisons and weapons she obtained with a skeleton key stolen from the Superintendent's office."

"Ah, I see. So, this girl was the murderer because she was discovered to be the secret supplier of the murder weapons?"

"Not quite. That's what I believed. However, my other assistant, Mrs. Elizabeth Packard, talked at length with this girl and discovered she had been mentally programmed and drugged by Dr.

Rooney and Galton, who were performing experiments on the five patients. The girl was actually attempting to do the bidding of an imaginary phantom, a devil figure, if you will."

Detective Abercrombie shook his head.

"Still one more conundrum to reveal the underlying truth. I find this happens quite often in my own cases. That is why we must act in an orderly and systematic manner. First, we ascertain how the victims died. Then, we can interview the seven suspects."

"Seven? How do you know there are seven?"

"Seven visitors came to the jail while you were traveling on the train. As you now know, their conversations with the deceased were transcribed, word-for-word, by the other victim, Officer Erin Scully. It is odd, but I noticed that my matron and the prisoner seemed to have an unusual affinity. It was most mysterious."

When Abercrombie stood up, she did as well.

"Where is your telephone? Dr. McFarland is at the Willard Hotel on Pennsylvania Avenue."

"It's with the Desk Sergeant. I shall meet you outside in my buggy. I advise you not to talk to any members of the press. Once we get specifics on the causes of death, we can parcel out details to our benefit."

She followed Detective Abercrombie out the door. She understood the warning about getting the press involved at this early stage in a murder investigation. Isaiah called journalists "the circus" because they were always after the most exciting angle to place in the center ring of their newspapers. Excitement for readers usually meant false rumors for criminal investigators.

***

Providence Hospital, between 2nd and 3rd St. and D and E St. Southeast.

The toxicology analysis for the Metropolitan Police was done at the Catholic hospital in the Southeast section of Washington, D. C. It also served as a morgue and the location for any injured or ailing prisoners of the jail.

As she and Dr. McFarland rode with Detective Abercrombie out to the hospital, she explained to her friend and associate what had occurred thus far. McFarland agreed that the bodies needed to be examined and their blood analyzed for poisons. It must be established that both drank from the bottle. Thus, the blood had to be analyzed to prove toxicity and death from the same poison.

However, as they were walking together into the main entrance of the hospital, Dr. McFarland stopped them with his raised hand. At sixty-four, he stood tall and straight, with gray, curly hair and a ruddy, Irishman's complexion.

"What were the other gifts from the visitors? We need to prove the poison was delivered through the brandy. However, it may have been transmitted by other means."

She watched as the short detective looked up at the taller doctor, and covered his eyes with his right hand, to see him better in the bright afternoon sunlight.

"That's quite astute of you. Let me see."

He pulled out the list from his suit coat pocket.

"The six other gifts were an Angel's Trumpet plant, a box of tea bags, perfume, a book on witchcraft, honey and apples, and corn bread. I can affix the visitors' names at a later time."

McFarland rubbed his chin.

"Any of those gifts could have transferred a poison to both victims, except for the flower plant and the book, of course."

"Will it take long to do the analysis? We can't interview the suspects until we know what killed our victims. I have never had a case like this one, so I am anxious to proceed."

She watched Abercrombie as he flexed his calves and raised up on his toes.

Dr. McFarland kept his voice even, possibly to assuage the younger man's anxiety.

"It depends. If it's in the blood, it should take more than an hour or so. But some poisons work in other organs, such as the brain, the liver, or the pancreas. That would extend the time by quite a bit. A day or possibly longer."

"I shall introduce you to our coroner, Dr. Fitzpatrick. While you work on the analysis, I want to take Mrs. Foltz to the canteen so we can discuss our possible strategies. Dr. Fitz can escort you to us when you've finished."

Dr. McFarland nodded.

"Yes, I look forward to discovering the cause of these poor ladies' deaths. Clara was very much looking forward to saving the life of Eloise Strong. But one cannot be certain of anything, as I have discovered over the years. Don't you agree, detective?"

"I do agree. I am fond of saying that the only definite event is change. At times, a different conundrum can be found around almost every corner. Let us proceed inside to circumnavigate a few corners, shall we?"

It took Detective Abercrombie about fifteen minutes to show Dr. McFarland where the basement morgue was located. She was waiting for him, a cup of tea in front of her, sitting at a table in the lunch canteen on the first floor. There were Negro women serving the food and drinks, and she could also see nuns outside the wide doors, in the passageway, going to a fro to accomplish their daily rounds.

Abercrombie came at her from the side, and she could see a large crucifix behind him on the wall. She, a Protestant, had always been fascinated by the Catholic crucifix, as it had the tortured Jesus dying upon it. Her father, a minister, had always mentioned that one of the major differences between the Protestant and Catholic beliefs was the Mass.

In the Catholic Mass, the bread was believed to be literally transubstantiated into the body of our Savior, and the wine became His blood. She had always envisioned this as a rather ghastly miracle, if indeed it was miraculous.

"Are you a religious man, Mr. Abercrombie?"

She spoke as the detective sat down across from her in another cushioned chair.

"Would you think me immoral if I said no?"

She noticed a slight squinting of his narrow eyes.

"Of course not. Human morality is not, in my mind, dictated by religious dogma. Look what our so-called Christian nation has done to the Natives and to your people, for example. All in the name of saving one's soul from perdition. No, I was just saying my own private prayer because of these horrific deaths. My father is both a lawyer and a minister, so I believe I have two sides of the fence covered. I feel doubly guilty, usually."

She watched him laugh, and it was a loud, robust chuckle. She enjoyed it.

"It is my turn to say that I like *you*, Mrs. Foltz. So many of my own people, as you call them, are deeply religious, and it often gets in the way of my investigations. Speaking of which, shall we go over the list of seven visitors?"

"By all means. The sooner we plot our strategy the sooner it will have to be changed."

She smiled, folded her hands on the table, and waited as he took out his paper.

"All right. After I read their names, I shall allow you to read the dialogues that were transcribed by Matron Scully. May 5, Frederick Douglas. May 6, Attorney General, Augustus Garland. May 7, Moses Fleetwood Walker. May 8, Sarah Bernhardt."

"The international actress? The Divine Sarah, as my son calls her?"

She was enthused.

"The very same. May 9, journalist and former congressman, Henry Watterson. May 10, First Lady Frances Cleveland. And, on May 11, Caroline Taylor, President of the Women's Christian Union."

Abercrombie handed the sheets to her, and she glanced over the names again.

"Mr. Douglas, a famous civil rights advocate, and one of the foremost promoters of women's suffrage I have ever read about. The President's Attorney General. A world-famous actress. And so on. You can't believe they all warrant suspicion, can you?"

"As you must know, even in the stories of Edgar Allan Poe, at the beginning of a mystery, everyone must be under suspicion. And, because these visitors were the last humans, we know of, who talked with both of our victims, they must indeed be suspected. Until we question them, and they can be proved to be without motive or means."

She noticed that Abercrombie had the same tenaciousness that her lover, Captain Lees possessed. She decided to become feline and play with him a bit longer.

"Quite. That means, of course, you must also be a suspect at this juncture. You visited the two victims, did you not?"

He smiled at her.

"Of course! Now you're understanding the methodology of the game. In fact, I am now going to tell you the first major clue, which may, coincidentally, also give me an alibi."

"Oh yes? Please do."

She leaned forward.

"On each of those days, I was logged out of the jail, and not present at all. I was giving a training class to police recruits on how to interact with Negroes during street patrols."

"And, how is that a clue in this case?"

"My assistant, Sergeant Bartholomew Hayes, fed the prisoner and looked in on her and Matron Scully each of those visiting days. He also escorted the visitors to and from the cell. We shall place him on our list as well. I dare say, he may have noticed something unusual about the behaviors of our visitors and of the two victims."

"Excellent. You are a fine detective. I look forward to working with you."

She saw him look up, so she turned around in her chair to see Dr. McFarland coming toward them from the canteen's entrance. He was not smiling. When he sat down, he did so with a slight exhale of disappointment.

"I have bad news. Nothing in the blood showed poison. Therefore, we shall be at it at least for the day, and possibly more. Your coroner was able to ascertain the times of death, however. Both victims, it seems, despite being in separate locales, died approximately within ten minutes of each other. At 0915, on Thursday, May 12."

The first "conundrum," as Abercrombie termed it, came at

them in the form of a tall, goateed gentleman, wearing a tailored, brown tweed suit and vest. He looked to be in his forties, with a full head of curly, blond hair under his stiff-crowned brown hat with the side brims turned up.

Without introducing himself, he sat down in one of the two remaining chairs at their table. As was usual with men, he addressed another male.

"I am so happy to find you, Dr. McFarland. When I heard the news about Eloise Strong, I read the article in the *Post* about you being in Washington to examine her for an insanity defense. The article mentioned you were staying at the Willard, so I first went there. They said you had come here with attorney Foltz." He nodded at her and touched his fingertips to his hat's brim. "Madam. I am the editor of the *Louisville Courier-Journal*. Henry Watterson." He turned back to Dr. McFarland. "Did she kill herself? Was she despondent over the death of her lover, Judge Owens?"

She watched Detective Abercrombie's face. The scar tissue turned a darker shade of pink before he exploded.

"Watterson! I am conducting a private investigation. How dare you insinuate your bloodhound nose into this case. You know the rules in this town."

Mr. Watterson, one on the list of seven suspects, briefly turned toward Abercrombie and smiled. He also twisted his mustache with his right thumb and forefinger and spoke with a polite, Southern drawl.

"Detective Abercrombie. My good sir. I have some detective work of my own to share with you, if you would be kind enough to stifle the smokehouse going on inside your head. But first, introduce me to this lovely young lady."

She could feel his deep blue eyes as they riveted upon hers. She had read the recent gossip by the Republicans concerning his rumored romance with the young First Lady. Watterson was married with several children back in his old Kentucky home. He was born in Washington D. C., so his editorial column, *Marse Henry*, was mostly taken up with gossip and news about the Capitol and its politicians.

"This is Mrs. Clara Shortridge Foltz. She was Miss Strong's defense attorney, but now she's assisting me in this investigation."

Abercrombie's words, she noted, were clipped and formal.

Again, Watterson reached for his hat, and, this time, he brought it completely off his head, and his smile could have been used to sweeten her tea.

"Miriam Levine, Mr. Garland's assistant, has told me so much about you. I was planning on writing about your work in my column. It is now being distributed in seventeen states through the Associate Press."

"Mr. Watterson, if you please," the detective interrupted. "Tell us your important news. I will be interviewing you about this case later, but we need to learn some scientific facts first."

Detective Abercrombie was being sparse with his own information, she noted.

"Very well, I shall inform you, if you promise to include me in your closed circle of detective work. I promise you, as a Southern gentleman, not to divulge a word until you give me approval."

Abercrombie looked down at his hands, and then he looked up at Watterson.

"Good. I will keep you in the loop, especially if your present information proves to be valuable to us."

"My sources in the South informed me that the baseball player, Moses Walker, had spoken ill of Judge Owens, whom he suspected was behind the banning of Negro athletes from the Major Leagues. I traveled to Newark, where Walker was catching in the International League in 1886 and this year."

"Mr. Walker visited the deceased Miss Strong in jail." Abercrombie pointed out.

"Now that makes sense. Because, according to the players I interviewed on his team, Walker wanted to seek retribution from Owens. You see, Walker was becoming quite a sensation on his team with his battery mate, a mulatto pitcher named George Stovey. Stovey won 33 games, and Walker had career highs in games played and batting average."

"Get to the point, Mr. Watterson. What did his teammates

say?" The detective struck her leg under the table with his nervous bouncing. "Excuse me, Mrs. Foltz."

"They said Walker told them he was going to get him and Stovey into the Major Leagues, and he was not going to let Judge Owens prevent it."

"I can see how that may relate to the murder of Owens, but how does this apply to the death of Miss Strong and Miss Scully?"

"The players found out that Walker was working with a Newark gang leader, Dante Cross, who had financed the first Negro minor league, the National Colored Baseball League, which ended abruptly because of lack of attendance. Cross often went to Washington D. C. and frequently hired the services of Miss Strong, *in flagrante*."

Abercrombie leaned forward.

"That is quite interesting. Continue."

Watterson also leaned forward. She knew he was coming in for the grand finale to his story.

"Cross supposedly told Walker that if he could get rid of Owens, then it would open up the Major Leagues to the coloreds. However, when Walker, Stovey and their Newark Giants were about to play the Chicago White Sox again, Cap Anson finally put his foot down and refused to take the field with the two darkies playing as the battery. Cross thought this game would open the door, but it was now closed to any colored man who wanted to join the Major Leagues. Even though Owens was dead, the owners would not budge because they witnessed the low attendance of the new colored league."

Abercrombie stiffened. "Do you mean you believe Walker was helping Cross and his gambling interests?"

"Yes. And, when your Miss Strong performed her murder, and it did not work out very well for Cross and his gangland activities, then Cross, most likely, sent Walker undercover as an educational ambassador to Washington to get even with her."

She watched, as Watterson leaned back in his chair, took a cigar from his coat pocket, and placed it between his lips. He then took out a box of wooden matches, extracted one, and swiped it across the table. He brought the blazing end to the tip of his pre-cut Cuban, and started to puff, sending clouds of gray smoke circling above their heads.

Chapter 6: Ford's Theater Redux

Willard Hotel, 1401 Pennsylvania Ave. NW, Washington, D. C., May 12, 1887.

When Madame Sarah Bernhardt telephoned their room at the hotel, David later explained to Laura that it was an "act of divine providence." He also pointed out that there were no coincidences. Everything was meant to be, and it was up to us to explain the connections.

They were about to travel to the first of two Washington destinations David Milton wanted to see. The initial visit was to be the Army Medical Museum, which, on April 14, 1865, was Ford's Theater, the location of the assassination of President Abraham Lincoln by the actor, John Wilkes Booth. She, who preferred visiting national monuments, art galleries, and libraries had difficulty understanding David's strange tastes and peculiarities.

She answered the monstrosity called a telephone, having been instructed on its use by the hotel's bell man. The communication device had not yet infiltrated San Francisco the way it had in the nation's capital, and she had never used one.

Awkwardly introducing herself as Laura de Force Gordon, by speaking into the black receiver, she felt as if she were awaiting a voice from the spirit world. In her earlier life, she had, indeed, portrayed a fictional spiritualist medium, to make money, but this was a phantasm made real by that scientific inventor, Alexander Graham Bell.

Bonjour, Miss Gordon, this is Sarah Bernhardt. Do you know where the attorney, Clara Shortridge Foltz, might be at present?

She stared down at the ear piece of the receiver in her hand. This voice was duplicating a French accent. She was astounded, not only because the voice sounded real, but also because it was telling her it was connected to the world's most renowned actress. Her better logic told her it could not be a disembodied spirit. Therefore, she informed the voice that she did know Clara and that her friend was presently not available.

"I am Mrs. Foltz's law partner," she explained, not knowing what to look at in the room as she spoke, so she focused on a Chinese vase sitting on the mahogany telephone table. The otherworldly practice of speaking to a voice without a body was quite infuriating to her sense of order.

The famous voice continued to say that she had just read about the death of Miss Eloise Strong in the morning edition of the *Washington Post*. Bernhardt explained that she had previously visited the young woman at the D. C. Jail on May 8.

She then explained to "Sarah," as Bernhardt insisted that she call her by her first name, that Clara was presently at that same jail, and that this news would be quite shocking to her.

"In the interim, I am caring for Clara's sixteen-year-old son, David Milton. We are taking the young man to visit the Army's Medical Museum previously called Ford's Theater."

Surprisingly, Sarah, the voice, said she had also done some sleuthing with the gendarmes in Paris. The actress said it helped her to portray mystery drama with more authenticity.

I believe the death of Eloise Strong might be a case of murder.

When she heard this statement, she immediately wished she were with Clara rather than supervising her son and listening to disembodied actresses. She looked over at David, who was now standing next to her and looking up, as he was a head shorter. After overhearing his name and Sarah's being mentioned, David asked her who was on the telephone, and when she whispered "Sarah Bernhardt," he began to screech at a high volume and leap into the air.

The impetuous boy was wearing a floral *cheongsam* he had borrowed from Ah Toy. He also wore rouge and dark eye shadow that his future sister-in-law, Adeline Quantrill, the psychic, showed him how to apply before they left San Francisco. His curly-brown hair had a reddish tint, like his mother's, and he had a feminine beauty that belied his natural gender.

When Sarah asked her what that "banshee noise" was, she

explained that it was Clara's son and that he was, quite possibly, the most informed follower of the actress on the West Coast and possibly in the world. Sarah quickly asked to speak to the boy, so she handed the receiver to David, happy to be rid of it.

She watched him grasp the device, and stare at it also, as if it were melting into his hand.

"Um, hello?" David mumbled in a hoarse whisper, after holding the receiver to his ear. She noted that he was also doing a jig on the Persian carpet.

The boy was so entranced listening to the actress that when he finished, after mumbling "yes," and hanging up, he told her he was now able to recite the performer's words verbatim. He obviously possessed his mother's almost photographic memory.

She then watched, in mesmerized fascination, as David pantomimed his idol, and pranced around the hotel room, flailing his hands about dramatically, and raising his eyebrows to create a variety of emotional expressions on his handsome young face.

"*Monsieur* Foltz? This is Sarah Bernhardt. I've been informed you are quite an avuncular fanatic of the thespian arts. I am going to be playing a challenging and controversial role in this afternoon's matinee at the National Theater. I would love to have you backstage as my guest. Also, Laura has told me you are visiting Ford's Theater this morning. May I meet you there to gain your insights? We could have *le déjeuner* afterward, no?"

She noticed that David was able to duplicate his idol's French accent very well.

When she received the second call, this one from Clara about the death of their client, Eloise Strong, she was an old hand at answering telephones. Clara quickly explained to her that she and Dr. McFarland would be on the murder case with Detective Hubert Abercrombie of the D. C. Jail. She also requested that she care for David Milton and take him wherever in Washington he wished to go.

She told her friend that Captain Lees had already purchased tickets for the three of them to attend the National Theater to see Sarah Bernhardt perform later that afternoon. She also explained that the famous actress had called to speak with Clara about the murder of Miss Strong.

What then resulted, she reported, was that Miss Bernhardt invited David Milton to be her guest backstage at the theater. She would also be meeting them at the Army Medical Museum this morning, and would be having lunch with them afterward, before going to the play. Clara replied that she would be busy on the case all day and that she would meet them back at the hotel for dinner that evening.

Following the call from Clara, she was instructed by the boy, in no uncertain terms, that the haunted building, even though it was no longer a theater, held so many evil spirits and enchanted magnetism within its confines that he knew he could become infused with supernatural power.

David further explained to her that he would thus become "sufficiently exotic" for when he viewed his idol, the Divine Sarah, at the play. She was beginning to wish the boy were with his mother and the alienist. Having never had children, she was quite wary of such unconventional activities.

She lived her life in an orderly, scientific manner. Supervising a boy like David was far beyond her capacity for what she viewed as frivolous logic. She did not judge the boy. She was as liberal minded as Clara in these matters, and she had learned a great deal about mental illness by participating in their recent investigation of the Stockton State Insane Asylum. But when one must be held responsible for a child's behavior, the Chinese silk slipper (two of which the boy was wearing) was on the other foot.

"Laura, are you all right? Who is in there with you?"

It was another disembodied voice; this time, it was coming from outside the hotel room. She knew it was Captain Lees' baritone. When she opened the door, his tall figure was filling the doorway, his right hand on the pearl handle of the Colt 45 holstered around his waist. She was happy to be back in the material, if perhaps more brutal, world.

"We are quite well. Just more of David's histrionics, I fear. We need to go now. I have a great deal to tell you on the carriage ride."

* * *

The Army Medical Museum, 511 10th St. NW, Washington, D.C.

As he gazed up at the facade of the Army Medical Museum, David Milton did not see a museum. He saw the repository of his wounded father's soul. The previous site, the theater where the Civil War president died, meant nothing to him. He knew his father's legal pension documents were stored here, somewhere on these first two floors, and they alone contained what was left of Jerimiah Foltz's will to live.

His father wrote to him every day, and his fierce but often deranged honesty was absorbed into the sixteen-year-old's consciousness like a drug. The more mysterious and alienated his father sounded, the more David turned to the world of drama and the theater. After memorizing them, he ritually burned the letters inside the Hopkins mansion's small observatory.

This was the room where his mother once hid her kidnapped Chinatown client, George Kwong, who would have been hanged had they not taken the risk. Keeping the content of his father's letters from his mother was also a risk, but he cherished them the same way his mother cherished the law.

Above him, he could see the dirty, third floor windows inside of which were the medical and human remains memorabilia. The macabre collection was kept by that same government--his father's worst nemesis. He was searching for a possible way to make connections in his mind to his father and to his mental and physical wounds.

Perhaps he could find an exhibit that would give him the key to curing his father of his deep depressions, and his frequent visits to the tavern or to the town hall, where he would shout at the bartender or the politician, whomever would listen, to increase the amount of money in his war pension.

He knew that his father's connections to the bartender and to the politician were the same. They were like David's connections to the theater and to life itself. Theirs was an absurd belief in the power of drama. The theater of war and the theater of the stage created magical connections, devoid of the legalistic logic and mumbo-jumbo of his mother and her friends, and more in tune with the person of Sarah Bernhardt, whose carriage was now rolling toward him, through the cacophony of street traffic, and stopping at the curb.

She was seated straight and proper inside the back of the red carriage, drawn by two Palomino stallions, and her dark eyes attached to his like two magnets. He froze in place on the sidewalk. Other pedestrians stopped to watch, but he was oblivious to them.

When the driver finally jumped down to open her door, his amazed eyes took in her costume. She wore the Elizabethan attire of a young man. He knew at once it was Hamlet, the young Prince of Denmark.

Her wig was short, in a page boy, the bangs covering her forehead. The sleeves of her tan blouse were puffy, with a high collar, and the bottom was lined with furry-white ermine. Her leotards were dark-brown and the boots long, seven-league-style black leather. She also had a sword attached to her waist on a copper-studded black belt, and her hat was a floppy brown affair, with a small bird's feather in the band.

He felt like his Chinese dress was ridiculous next to her flamboyant attire, but she came up to him, nonetheless, intuiting that it was he who was the strange boy on the telephone. He was particularly entranced with her greeting because both Laura Gordon and Captain Lees were left standing together, watching them both as they hugged. Divine Sarah kissed both of his cheeks, and the touch of her soft lips radiated throughout his body like an electric shock.

"*Monsieur* David. I am not playing Prince Hamlet. This afternoon, at the National Theater, I am the Princess Fédora Romazov."

Her voice was, indeed, a golden shower of enunciated beauty. She took his hand in hers.

"However, I thought it proper to come as the teenage prince, as we will tour the medical museum, no? Perhaps Yorick's skull is inside to teach us about mortality."

Her touch gave him courage. "I think perhaps Yorick, the king's favorite jester, would also wear a fedora, if the Russian princess did."

"*Mais oui! Absolument!* Your wit rivals the Czar of Russia in its eloquent humor."

He watched Laura move toward them.

"Sarah, I am the body attached to the voice with whom you spoke earlier. Attorney Laura de Force Gordon. We are so honored that you could take the time to visit with David. And this is Captain Isaiah Lees of the San Francisco Police Department."

Laura turned back toward her comrade, and he noticed that tall Captain Lees was a bit star-struck as well, as he did not move an inch. Lees nodded twice, but his bushy eyebrows were raised, instead of in a downward scowl, which was his usual expression.

"Shall we go in?"

Sarah grabbed him by the crook of his arm. His heart began to pound, as he led her to the entrance of the museum. Laura and Captain Lees followed close behind.

"It smells like old papers in here," Captain Lees said, as they took the slow visitors' elevator up to the third floor. There were five other people inside, and he noticed they were all casting sideways glances at Sarah and him.

"I read where this museum had over thirty thousand visitors last year. And the library had five hundred readers."

Laura was her usual informative self.

He wished Bertha May, his sister, were there to share the more enchanted aspects of the visit. However, as he glanced over at the Divine Sarah, he noted that her gaze was wistful and expectantly aware.

"My father fought in the war," he told her. "He was wounded in the shoulder and leg at the Battle of Chickamauga, under General William Rosecrans. It was in Georgia, and it had the second highest number of casualties of the war other than Gettysburg. Everybody remembers Gettysburg because it was the last battle."

"I fought under Sherman, and we pressed on into Atlanta. Many fine men—on both sides—lost their lives," Captain Lees said.

"I read in the museum brochure that they have many of the surgical instruments used and invented during the war." Laura glanced down at her brochure. "All the exhibits are numbered so you can match them with further information inside the pamphlet."

The elevator operator stopped the carriage at their floor, and the doors swung open. Hamlet, his companion, darted out into the exhibit like a spring lamb. He followed her. They had no brochure, no numbers to track down. Only their fertile imaginations to give them a mystical compass.

"Look, David! I am Sergeant McCandless. I lost my legs at Chickamauga, and they gave me these wooden ones."

Sarah was walking stiffly on the tiles, ignoring the exhibits in their glass cases lined on both sides of the wide floor. In the center of the room were an assortment of tables that held a variety of skulls, legs and other body parts from whatever corpses they once were a part.

"When I was attending a séance in the moonlight, last evening, there appeared to me a most curious sight. I looked closely, and what appeared were my two lost limbs, stored here in this museum!"

Sarah began to stagger, almost falling against one of the tables.

"What's wrong, sergeant?" He called after her.

She turned around and stared at him, shaking first her right leg and then her left.

"My legs, of course! They've been kept in alcohol all these years, and when their spirits possessed my wooden ones, I began to walk with the drunken gait of a sailor on liberty!"

Sarah laughed, and when she did, dozens of other tourists began to laugh as well. Her golden voice had attracted a small audience.

He felt jubilant for the first time in many days. He at last had an adult who understood what it meant to be spontaneous and quick-witted.

In order to go along with their impromptu play, he rushed over to one of the skulls exhibited on a table. He ignored the sign which stated that this was "the skull of assassin Lewis Powell, who attacked Secretary of State William Seward," with number 2244 stamped on his bone forehead. He picked it up and took the stance of Sarah's character, the noble Prince of Denmark. He held the skull in his right palm, with his right arm stretched out, and his left hand poised at the palm on his left hip. He stared down at the skull in deep contemplation.

"What good is your Army pension now, you poor bloke? This might be the pate of a politician, which this ass now o'er-reaches; one that would circumvent God, might it not?"

Sarah walked over to him, drunkenly, on her two imaginary wooden legs, and took up the refrain. She pointed to a skull on a different table.

"There's another. Why may not that be the skull of a lawyer? Where be his quiddities now, his quillets, his cases, his tenures, and his tricks? Why does he suffer this rude knave now to knock him about the sconce with a dirty shovel, and will not tell him of his action of battery? Hum!"

He noticed that Laura was frowning, and yet he was enjoying the experience immensely. Captain Lees was also chuckling until his belly shook.

He sensed that Divine Sarah had a grand finale in mind. She moved quickly to pose; her head was thrust forward in one of her stock dramatic stances. She unsheathed her sword, holding it aloft so that the sun's light pouring in from the ceiling transoms of colored glass reflected off the blade in a dazzling glitter.

The prince pointed the sword at the skull in David's hand.

"Alas, poor Yorick! I knew him, Horatio: a fellow of infinite jest, of most excellent fancy."

Taking the clue, he moved over to stand next to the beautiful prince, turning the white skull over and over in his hands as the drama continued. The entire tourist community had now formed a circle around them, peering with fascination and quizzical embarrassment, to see such folly inside a medical museum for the

United States Army.

The prince was standing behind Captain Lees, and she rushed up to him, took him by his broad shoulders, and jumped upon his back, grasping her sword in her left hand, and wrapping her right hand around his neck to grab his chest.

"He hath borne me on his back a thousand times; and now, how abhorred in my imagination it is!"

Captain Lees, finally getting into the act, began to lope, in a circle, with Sarah Bernhardt on his back. He ran alongside them, thrusting the skull of the assassin of the Secretary of State up to her face as she continued her soliloquy.

"Here hung those lips that I have kissed I know not how oft." She kissed the captain's cheek. "Where be your gibes now?"

He was thinking of his father, Jeremiah, and how fearful he was about allowing that hardened soldier of the Union to see how much he had changed. He was now this provocative youth, this mad and frolicsome youngster, who enjoyed watching the bodies of other, like-minded and free-spirited males and females.

At this moment, he did not care. He was elated by a bold actress, his idol, and by the acceptance of these two other adults. Divine Sarah was waiting for him, riding her steed around and around. He was following, holding up the skull of Yorick, Lewis Powell, Jeremiah Foltz, perhaps humanity itself. He saw that Laura was laughing, so he completed the refrain from memory.

"Your gambols? Your songs? Your flashes of merriment, that were wont to set the table on a roar? Not one now, to mock your own grinning? Quite chap-fallen?"

As he finished the refrain, Captain Lees fell to the floor of the Army Medical Museum, the Divine Sarah with him, and the people were laughing, sending cascades of jolly humor throughout the grim displays of bodies, bones, and macabre utensils of battlefield salvation.

All that he could think about was his father taking him to bed that last time; and he, riding his back; an eight-year-old boy's legs wrapped around that hard and unreachable torso, and his child's mind became enveloped in the mystery of an adult's defeat inside a small boy's apparent victory.

National Theater, 1321 Pennsylvania Avenue, NW, Washington, D. C., 8 PM.

David was allowed to order any item on the luncheon menu he desired. He told the others all he wanted was a baguette and Roquefort cheese spread. He was too excited about going to the theater to eat much. He also ignored most of the adult luncheon conversation. Instead, he went over in his mind the last letter from his father.

I hope you can visit this summer, David. I believe if I take you with me to the Office of Veterans' Affairs, I may be able to convince them of my need. You are such a good actor! We can convince them that my mind is not stable. My injuries are such that my pension should be increased three-fold, don't you agree?

All he knew about his father's pension was that he received ten dollars per month for his injuries and that his mental health was not good. Jerimiah was an enlisted man during the war, and now he did not work. He had no children in his second marriage to a much younger woman, a nurse named Katherine Gadfry, from San Jose.

He was the only one of his brother and sisters who still communicated with his father. His three sisters and brother blamed their father for leaving their mother with five children for a younger woman. When President Cleveland vetoed one hundred pension bills in February, he began to notice that his father's letters were sounding more desperate.

The only family conversations about the law that he paid any attention to were the ones concerning veterans. His mother and Laura believed, along with the current president, that the vetoes of the hundreds of private pension bills that came up through the liberal congress were to stop greedy methods of getting money by fraudulent means. His mother, especially, held a personal resentment about his father's desertion, and her voice became filled with rancor. She gave the same speech, in different forms, many times over the years.

"Jerimiah refused to work, even though he made time for the tavern. He made no effort to help me with the children, and I had to borrow money from my father, as my teacher's salary was not enough. When he left me for that woman, I vowed to never be dependent on any man ever again!"

This was the statement that made his sympathy toward his father real. When he heard his mother say this, he made his own vow. He would do whatever he could to help his father survive in a country that refused to acknowledge the disabilities caused by the war that they started.

He read about the war until late in the evenings. The rich men could get out of serving by paying other men three hundred dollars to take their places. President Cleveland, in fact, had been one such man. This had caused riots in New York City. When the war ended, his father received only five dollars per month because the government did not recognize Jerimiah's mental problems caused by the war. And today, the president was forbidding any type of pension to save money and to make himself appear to be thrifty and resolute to the people, like his mother, who had voted him into office in 1886.

***

Later that evening, as he watched Divine Sarah playing Princess Romazov, from the wings of the National Theater, he believed, for the first time, that he could also become an actor. He would gain fame and fortune to help his father get out of debt and live a decent life. Like his idol, he would play both male and female characters. Nothing was impossible in the world of art and drama, and his heart filled with joy at the prospect.

The odors of greasepaint, tobacco, perfumes and sweat mixed in that darkness, where the lights shined upon you standing on the stage, and the audience was held, in a transfixed state of wonderment and rapture, as you created a world of costumes, colors and invented, yet very meaningful, dialogues. It was all a creative world, far beyond the realities of wars and the real damage they caused.

He felt the hand on his mouth, and he tasted the bitterness on the cloth before he could smell it. When he could finally breathe, his wide eyes noted, with interest, that onstage, Princess Romazov was reclining on her divan. The wrist of her right hand was at her forehead, and she was sighing for her lost love.

His body relaxed along with her, and he could not move. The cloth was still being held over his nose and mouth.

That was when he remembered that his idol had once played Judas Iscariot. In the play, Judas was angry at Jesus because he had stolen Mary Magdalene, who was the lover of both Judas and Pontius Pilot.

Who is angry at me?

That was the last thing he remembered. The darkness enveloped him in its comfort, as the strong arms lifted him into the throes of despair.

Chapter 7: Nightmares

Willard Hotel, 1401 Pennsylvania Ave. NW, Washington, D. C., May 12, 1887, 8 PM.

Clara's nightmare began when Captain Lees called her at the hospital. Her son, David Milton, had vanished during the stage play at the National Theater. He told her that he was going to accompany Sarah Bernhardt in a search of the theater and nearby buildings. The actress felt personally responsible for the boy's disappearance. Laura was returning to the hotel to meet her.

She was so emotionally distraught that all three men who were with her at Providence Hospital, Detective Abercrombie, Dr. McFarland, and Henry Watterson, decided to accompany her back to the hotel. The Coroner, Dr. Fitzpatrick, told Abercrombie that he would certainly call the hotel when he finally determined the poison or other causes of the Strong and Scully deaths.

On the ride over, she explained to the men about her son's love of the theater and drama. In addition, she said he had been hurt the most by his father leaving the family. She wanted to believe that he may have even decided to go off on his own to explore. He had done it once before, in San Francisco, when he had failed in three of his high school classes.

The men agreed that he was probably testing his independence, in that he was sixteen and full of what Dr. McFarland termed the "imaginary audience." She understood when the doctor further explained that adolescents develop a personal fable. They believe that their thoughts, feelings and experiences are exclusively distinct, more terrible, and more exceptional than others'. She knew that was certainly her son's behavior, especially as of late.

Laura hugged her when she stepped through the door. After she quickly introduced her friend to the two unknown men, Laura began to relate the incidents of the day in her usual calm and determined manner. However, she did notice that her friend's voice contained an emotional quiver.

73

"David was in wonderful spirits at the Army Medical Museum. He and Sarah performed an improvised comedy with the exhibit's skulls, quoting from *Hamlet* and getting Captain Lees into the act. Sarah jumped on Isaiah's back and rode him like a horse. All the tourists enjoyed it immensely. He wasn't depressed at all the way he was on the train ride to Washington."

"Did he mention anything about his father?"

She was probing for reasons why David might disappear on his own.

"No. I would have to ask Sarah and Isaiah, but I don't believe so. Don't worry, Clara. I am certain he'll reappear. Most likely, he started talking with one of the actors backstage, and they decided to go somewhere."

Detective Abercrombie stepped forward.

"I can call the precinct in that area. They can search with your captain and do some forensics around the backstage area."

Her heart began to quicken. She could feel throbbing in her forehead. Usually, that meant a headache was imminent. She had yet to eat.

"Could we call room service? I need to eat something."

She moved to the telephone stand next to the couch.

Laura smiled.

"Good for you. I used that device today, and I am not enamored of the experience. It's rather like talking to my former husband. I could hear him talking, but nobody was really there."

Dr. McFarland tugged at his beard.

"Laura, you never cease to amaze me. When everyone else is serious, you can find humor. Usually, and Clara can attest to this, our own levity cannot make you laugh."

"What does everyone want?"

She reached for the pad and pencil next to the telephone. The phone began to ring, so she picked up the large black receiver instead.

"Detective Abercrombie? It's for you." She handed the telephone to him.

"Yes. Yes, we are. Nothing yet? All right. Do the other tests.

I will stop by the lab on my way back to the jail. Goodbye." The detective placed the telephone back on the cradle, but as soon as he did so, it rang again. "Shall I?" he asked, and she nodded for him to answer it.

She saw the expression on the scarred face of the policeman turn from inquisitive interest to shocked amazement. He said nothing for several moments. He picked up the notepad and pencil and wrote something down. He tore off the sheet of paper and held it. Finally, he squeezed the handle on the telephone and thrust his chin up.

"We are already on the case, commissioner. I do understand it becomes a higher priority. Yes. I can see your point. Correct. Yes, sir."

After he hung up, he turned to address the entire group.

"As they say in baseball, we now have a new ball game. That was President of the D. C. Board of Commissioners. Mr. William Benning Webb. First Lady Frances Cleveland was visiting the Home for Friendless Colored Girls on Meridian Hill. She left there, according to Mrs. Caroline Taylor, at seven this evening. Two female members of the Women's Christian Temperance Union, who were visiting taverns in Murder Bay with a policeman, discovered her buggy parked outside one of those taverns. Jasper Woodley, her Negro chauffer, was found unconscious, slumped over in the driver's seat. Mrs. Cleveland was nowhere to be found."

"Sounds like a kidnapping."

Henry Watterson was writing down something in a notepad he extracted from his coat pocket.

"President Cleveland has called upon the Maryland and Virginia state militias to assist in a house-to-house search. This will be in addition to the two hundred officers just assigned by Commissioner Webb. That's almost half of all the police in Washington."

"What are we supposed to do now?"

She needed to know.

"Mr. Webb knows about your boy, and he thinks the two events are related."

She noticed that the detective seemed to have a difficult time looking at her.

"Why is that?"

She did not want to know the answer.

"A poem was found tucked inside the watch pocket of the chauffeur. It said, and you must excuse me, ladies, for the crudeness of the language."

Abercrombie read from the paper in his hand. "'We got your nigger-lovin' Frankie, the White House toy. And the Jew-lovin' zanie, the Californy boy. Tell Big Steve he better open up his bank. Or else both these chickens are walkin' the plank.'"

She needed something to hold onto, as she was feeling quite faint. She moved over to Dr. McFarland and grasped his arm.

The alienist stared directly at the detective.

"I know the term zanie means homosexual. But who, pray tell is Big Steve?"

"Stephen Grover Cleveland is our president's full name. Back in New York, when he was governor, the opposition called him Big Steve or Uncle Jumbo." Abercrombie pointed out.

She walked over to the telephone and picked it up. She dialed room service.

"Hello? This is Mrs. Foltz in room 428. Could you bring up an assortment of sandwiches, non-alcoholic drinks, and accoutrements? Thank you."

She dropped the receiver into the cradle and walked back to the circle of four others.

"I believe we can make due with a smorgasbord at this point, don't you? The first item on our agenda is to assess what we do know. Let's sit around this table and discuss our plans, shall we?"

She was pleased to see the others follow her lead and sit down at the small conference table on the other side of the room, near the window. When everyone was arranged, she began.

"I don't want to sound too omniscient, but since my son has been placed in harm's way, I believe my stake in the outcome of this search is as primary as the president's."

Detective Abercrombie smiled at her.

"By all means, Mrs. Foltz. I believe it stands to reason. If these kidnappers have done their due diligence, then they must know your hotel room and telephone number. And, since the First Lady frequently had women, of all classes and colors, who visited her inside the White House, then we know they also must have planned her abduction for quite some time as well."

"I want to discuss Mr. Watterson's research into the gambler known as Dante Cross from Newark. It would seem that thread of inquiry fits best with the facts we now know. Agreed?"

She opened the top two buttons on the high collar of her green Parisian satin dress.

Mr. Watterson struck the table with his fist.

"She's right! This could certainly be all on one stick. I have another angle to add. When I visited your Miss Strong in jail, I told her about a group of Southern boys called Redshirts. They are bigots that threatened to kill anyone who supported her in any way."

Abercrombie nodded.

"Yes, the language used in that note was certainly bigoted and anti-Semitic."

Dr. McFarland cleared his throat.

"Ahem. The reference to the boy being a zanie would also mean they were familiar with buggery and perhaps even heshe child prostitutes."

"The fact that Frances Cleveland's buggy was found in the poor section of Washington would lend itself to that theory. I would assume plenty of prostitution and other criminal activities abound there."

She was happy to see that Laura was back to her attorney self.

"However, can we assume these kidnappers were both Southern bigots and Northern gangsters? That would seem to be quite a stretch of reason, no?"

She wanted the discussion to focus again.

The Negro detective shook his head.

"No, not that much of a stretch, Mrs. Foltz. Gangsters are often quite bigoted as well. It depends on the gang leader, in most instances."

The journalist Watterson got up when there was a knock at the door. She assumed that because he worked the political circuit in Washington, he was ever vigilant about the prospect of food. She watched, as the tall Watterson led the two waiters inside and showed them where to place the food, most of it next to his seat at the table.

After everyone had a turkey, chicken, or roast beef sandwich, and a cold drink, she wanted to plan things more carefully based on the reality of the police and military sweep of the city going on.

"I believe we must still interview the six people who visited Eloise Strong last week. We should start with Mr. Moses Walker due to the information Mr. Watterson gave us. If he admits knowing the gang leader, Dante Cross, then we may have a real suspect to pursue most diligently."

Abercrombie nodded.

"I agree. I shall accomplish that. I have more connections in the D. C. neighborhood wherein Mr. Walker would frequent. I can readily verify if the man has been seen contacting gang members. I also need to question my assistant jailer and stay in touch with Dr. Fitzpatrick about the cause of death of the two women."

"Good. I shall interview Mrs. Caroline Taylor at the Home for Friendless Colored Girls and Mr. Frederick Douglas. Laura, I would like you to talk to Augustus Garland and Sarah Bernhardt."

She wiped her mouth with the cloth napkin and stood up.

"Let us hope these ruffians can be found soon. Dr. McFarland, would you please man the hotel telephone? Something tells me these kidnappers will be contacting us. Money seems to be the prime objective."

Detective Abercrombie walked around the table to talk with her.

"The White House will be contacting your room about what the president and the police plan to say to these kidnappers. I would assume they will have men posted here, and at the White House, in case the kidnappers call."

"Thank you, Mr. Abercrombie. I know you said you were

not a religious man, but I would like to hold hands with you all. We may each think good thoughts or pray."

She held out her arms.

Everyone formed a circle, and they stood there for several moments, heads bowed. She became very solemn.

"Jesus, if you allow my son to be saved, I will make amends to Jerimiah and allow David to visit him. I have been much too selfish. Amen."

***

The Preparatory High School for Negroes, 2565 Georgia Avenue, N.W., Washington, D.C. May 12, 1887, 9:45 PM.

Moses was staying in a back room at the high school. After his visit to see Eloise Strong, he made the arrangement to stay in Washington to protect her. But now, after the news of Miss Strong's death and possible murder, and the kidnapping of the First Lady and a California white boy, the entire Negro community was in a panic. Mr. and Mrs. Terrell and Principal Cardozo told him the police would be there to question everyone, so he should be ready.

A storm began, and it was raining. He could see flashes of lightning through the one window which overlooked Howard Way.

When the short man in the inexpensive suit and dripping rain coat knocked on his door, and he opened it, the man's deformed face caused him such a fright that he slammed the door shut.

"Mr. Walker? I am here to ask you some questions."

He opened the door again. "I am so sorry. The darkness and storm when I answered the door."

"I understand. My appearance does that quite often. You may trust that I am not the killer from the Rue Morgue. I am Detective Hubert Abercrombie. Metropolitan Police. May I ask you some questions concerning the death of Miss Eloise Strong?"

"Certainly. Come in. The accommodations are sparse, but you may sit here."

He pulled out one of the two chairs from beneath a small card table. When the detective sat down, he pulled out the other one and sat next to him. As he stared at the man's face, he realized it was mostly scar tissue on a Negro's features.

"First, I would like to ask you about your visit to Miss Strong at the D. C. holding facility."

He watched the detective pull out some folded papers from his suit coat pocket. He opened them.

"The matron there, in case you failed to notice, kept a transcript of your dialogue with Miss Strong on May 7. I have that dialogue recorded here on these pages."

He tried, with some difficulty, to remember all that he discussed with Eloise Strong that day. He did remember promising to protect the young woman from any harm.

"I don't recall the matron, but I do remember my visit."

He attempted to keep his eyes on the ugly face of the detective, but he could not. He kept looking off to the side, and he knew that might look suspicious.

"It appears you wanted to become a lone vigilante. You stated that you would watch Miss Strong's comings and goings like the proverbial hawk watches a chicken. Were you angry when she died?"

"Angry? Why would I be angry? I was quite shocked, but my experience told me this was bound to happen."

"Does your experience also include extracurricular employment with a gentleman by the name of Cross? Dante Cross?"

He was expecting this line of questions at some point. Just this year, in March, he had met with Mr. Cross, as he was a major financial source for funds to begin the new National Colored Baseball League.

"Yes, I met with Mr. Cross three times in Newark. It was his idea to use the term Cuban for teams in the proposed new league. He knew many white people were bigots, so he said they were too stupid to realize the Negroes who played were not from Cuba but just plain old darkies."

He chuckled but noticed the detective was not smiling.

"But the league was not a good idea, now was it? You wanted to be in the big leagues, correct? The team you were on was there for a brief time, but then it was demoted again. Why was that?" The detective leaned forward. "You can tell me, brother. I will understand."

He believed the policeman.

"The judge who was murdered by Eloise Strong. Marshal Owens. He knew all the owners in the majors. He also knew some of the most bigoted players, like Cap Anson, the star of the White Sox. Dante Cross explained to me that when the Civil Rights Act of 1875 was ignored by the Supreme Court, in 1883, it gave the states the right to discriminate again. According to him, that's what doomed the Negro league."

"Do you think Cross doomed Judge Owens?"

He thought that was an interesting tactic.

"I believe Eloise Strong killed Judge Owens. Wasn't she the one having an affair with him?"

"Are you aware that Dante Cross is the leader of a criminal gang in Newark? According to my sources, he was also having an affair, as you term it, with Miss Strong."

He noted that the Negro detective chose this moment to smile.

"No. All I know about Cross is that he has the money to start a new league for my people who play baseball. The white bigots, like Judge Owens, were not allowing it. If I knew Cross was a gangster, I would have never met with him."

"Here's the way I see the murders playing out. First, Cross contracts Eloise Strong to knife Judge Owens at the Nationals' game. Then, when you told Dante Cross that she was going to tell authorities about this contract, he had her killed also. My matron, Erin Scully, just drank from the same poison, so to speak, and got in the way."

He stood up.

"Listen. I told you I never knew Cross was a gang leader. I was also not aware that Miss Strong knew him or was having any relations with him."

He watched the detective stand.

"Why did she tell you that she believed she was still a slave?

To me, that sounds quite similar to a master servant relationship, don't you agree?"

"Brother, I believe you need to take that up with the two persons who made the contract. Since one of them is dead, then I suggest you focus on Cross."

He moved over to the front door and opened it.

"I shall be doing just that, as a matter of fact, Mr. Walker. Don't go anywhere, as I may be contacting you with what I discover. If your information proves false, then my interest in you may escalate."

He shut the door behind the detective and leaned his back against it. He took three deep breaths. He expected the white demons to invade at any moment.

***

The White House, 1600 Pennsylvania Avenue. West Wing, Blue Room, May 13, 1887.

Laura had a problem getting an appointment with Attorney General Augustus Garland. The telephone in the White House had been commandeered by the Secret Service unit awaiting the call from the kidnappers. Once she was able to reach the President's Secretary, Daniel Lamont, through a Western Union message, he arranged the appointment for her at ten in the morning.

She decided to wear a more fashionable dress for the meeting. It was a gray, pleated affair accompanied by a round white-straw hat with gray band. It had a high collar, dark gray vest, and a medium bustle, which was quite different than her more plebeian, navy dresses, with no bustles, which she chose for court.

There were at least fourteen militiamen from Maryland on the front lawn of the White House, and she persevered through the coterie of men who searched her, from head to foot. She made only one remark, remonstrating a young man by asking if he would look up the pant legs of males who came to visit the White House, but her comment seemed to be lost to his officiousness and embarrassed demeanor, as he felt under her dress for weaponry. Indeed, she almost felt sorry for the poor lad.

As she was escorted by one of these militia to the Blue Room, she gazed at the portraiture of former presidents and other dignitaries hanging on the walls. Although it was certainly a high point in her career as an attorney, she focused upon the figure of the short man in the blue suit standing in the center of the room, his arms outstretched in a typically Southern greeting.

"Mrs. Gordon! How charmed to make your acquaintance. May I get us some cordials?"

She allowed him to take her two hands and guide her to one of the two padded leather chairs set in the middle of the room for their conference. Once Mr. Garland was seated, she reached into her purse and took out the copy of the transcripts that were taken during Garland's meeting at the jail with their former client, Eloise Strong.

"I believe time is certainly of the essence, so I will get right to my questions, if you don't mind, Mr. Attorney General."

He smiled and rubbed his hands together.

"By all means. As we are fellow attorneys, we both understand the value of time, to be billed by the hour, of course!"

"I understand your discovery evidence was quite substantial, but there was a comment Miss Strong made to you that confused me. She told you she was a child of God and not susceptible to the court's laws. Did you find that odd coming from a young woman who was seeking to become more educated in that same law?"

"Indeed, I did. In fact, during the questioning of persons who knew Miss Strong, we discovered that she was a very religious woman. However, I did not find her statements too odd, in that most former slaves have been found to be quite orthodox in their beliefs, no matter how much education they might have had. The church, you see, is one of the few paths to the wider community, especially in the South."

Garland leaned forward.

"Correct. Although, coming from a prostitute who was not averse to making her bed with strange fellows, might it not be possible she was rationalizing her actions?"

She wanted to get to the heart of her probing.

"People do change, attorney Gordon, despite what some people believe. I was a soldier of the Confederacy, but I also held pro-suffrage and anti-slave beliefs at the same time. I needed only the opportunity to make amends, once the war was over. Perhaps Miss Strong could have accomplished the same amends, had she not decided to take matters into her own hand, so to speak."

"Do you and the president believe the kidnapping of First Lady Frances Cleveland was connected to the murder of Judge Owens?"

She wanted to connect those two events, even though Clara and the others had not ventured in that direction as yet.

"We do not rule the connection out. We understand the acrimony of our political adversaries, and the recent coverage in the press of our president's wedding and romance may have hatched many strange ideas. We have been working on several theories, as a matter of fact. One of which includes you and Mrs. Foltz, to be honest."

He was no longer smiling.

Her temper was rising.

"Is that so? And, what might that theory be, good sir?"

"Your dark eyes are quite ravishing when you flare up. Everyone is suspect, you should be aware, at the start of an investigation. Until we get the call from these kidnappers, we have little to go on but speculation. Since you insist. You and your California team could make quite a stir by extorting the White House and kidnapping the First Lady. With your boy also in your custody, it would seem the best ruse to take us off your trail, would it not?"

She stood up.

"I don't believe we can successfully communicate at this point. I have another appointment. Please call the hotel when you do receive the call from our common foe. Good day to you, sir!"

She would have much preferred to use California suffragist bombast on this sorry excuse for a man, but she intuitively understood it would do no good. From what she had researched concerning Cleveland, Garland and Owens, they were all anti-suffrage, for their own purposes, of course, and Garland himself was lying to her about it. She wanted to get across town to meet with Sarah Bernhardt. She was getting nowhere questioning *this* Southern gentleman.

***

Home for Friendless Colored Girls, Erie Street, Meridian Hill, N.W., Washington, D. C., May 13, 1887.

Clara thought it was quite interesting that the police and state militias were searching all the houses in Washington, D. C., including those of the wealthy class. She had it in her mind that President Cleveland might have ordered his men to inspect the coloreds and those in Murder Bay first. His wife's buggy was discovered, after all, in the poor section, and it made sense to her to inspect that area right away. However, she was certainly not the president, and she had her own methods of investigation.

The Washington Meridian travels due north from the White House and continues right down the center of 16th Street, all the way to the Maryland line. Given its location, the hill was named Meridian Hill. The Meridian Hill section had many trees and natural foliage. The spring season brought the songs of birds and the rambunctious chases of squirrels and other animals.

The rented hansom cab driver was giving her a smooth ride, for the most part, down the center of the nation's capital. Out her window she saw, interspersed with nature, the marching platoons of quiet men in uniform, both Capitol police and Maryland troopers. She watched, as they broke ranks, their rifles bouncing against their backs, to spread out and enter all the homes in the area, including, she assumed, the domicile toward which she was now walking.

She had already interviewed Frederick Douglas the evening before, as he was available at his residence. The great civil rights and women's rights leader had little to say, other than he believed Miss Strong to be a victim of the increasing distrust of the Negro and women in America. He had not noticed any strange behavior by her on the day he visited the D. C. Jail.

This led her to believe the poison must have been in the

bottle of liquor that the First Lady had brought on May 10, and it wasn't of the slow acting variety. She did inquire about the Angel's Trumpet plant Mr. Douglas had brought with him. He told her he purchased it from a disabled war veteran outside the jail, before he entered.

That morning, the special pair of Secret Service agents had entered her hotel room to establish their stations to await the important call from the kidnappers. Dr. McFarland was allowed to answer the telephone, but he was instructed not to negotiate with them until they gave their parameters about the transfer and delivery of the hostages.

Before leaving the hotel, Detective Abercrombie had called her with some interesting news. Although Dr. Fitzpatrick, the coroner and medical examiner, had yet to determine the poison in the systems of the two women, he had done a complete autopsy of their corpses. There were no physical signs of forced trauma on either body, but there was a dark tattoo, about four inches tall, engraved upon the small of the back of each woman. It was an ornate depiction of a naked man, arms at his sides, with the wings of an angel and the head of a lion. Around his body, a snake was encircled, with its head pointing directly at the face of the roaring lion.

This was certainly an item she wanted to discuss with the group, especially with Dr. McFarland. It may signify that the women were members of some kind of group or cult. Or, perhaps they were both prostitutes, marked by a pimp or bawdy Madame for some financial purpose.

When she entered the Home for Friendless Colored Girls, she was met at the door by an armed soldier. He asked her for identification, and when she told him she wished to speak with Mrs. Caroline Taylor, the proprietor, he looked down at his boots and mumbled something.

"I'm sorry, but I can't hear you," she told him.

He finally raised his curly-brown head of hair and stared at her. His Maryland State Militia uniform appeared two sizes too large for him.

"I'm afraid Mrs. Taylor is dead, Mrs. Foltz. She hanged

herself. The coroner is over there."

He pointed toward an older gentleman with red hair, standing in the corner of the living room. The children had been taken out somewhere by the housekeeper.

"Dr. Fitzpatrick? Is that you?"

Having never met him at the hospital, she was acting on a hunch. There was one bit of information she wanted to know.

He turned toward her and motioned for her to come near him. She did so. When she mentioned Detective Abercrombie, he smiled and nodded.

"Elephant Man. You must be attorney Foltz."

She decided to ask her question and have done with it.

"Did you perform a cursory search of the body, by any chance, Dr. Fitz?"

She held her breath, waiting for the answer.

"That I did. And, yes, she had the same tattoo at the small of her back as the other two women. A lion-headed, flying snake man."

"I see. Could you perhaps perform a toxicology test on Mrs. Taylor similar to what you're doing on the Strong and Scully bodies? I wish to know if their deaths are connected in any way."

"Certainly. I'll call you when I have the results. Good day."

Dr. Fitzpatrick turned back to his business: the corpse suspended by a rope from the wood rafters above him.

When she left, she realized that the mystery was getting much deeper than she had at first anticipated. As she walked down the hill toward her cab, she was approached by an old man in tattered overalls. He had an enlisted man's Union Army cap and walked with a limp.

"Good mornin', mam. Could you have some coins to spare for an old veteran of Chickamauga?"

That was the battle where her Jerimiah was wounded. She extracted a quarter from her handbag and handed it to the man. She remembered that Frederick Douglas had also been approached by a disabled veteran before his visit to see Eloise Strong at the D. C. Jail. She knew these veterans were not being treated fairly by the present administration, which, in turn, caused them to seek other means, even begging, to gain income. Of course, there were also those, like Jerimiah, who relied solely upon the government, or their wives, for income. She did wonder, however, whether First Lady Cleveland had also met with a veteran before she visited Eloise Strong.

Chapter 8: Martial Law

*Willard Hotel, 1401 Pennsylvania Ave. NW, Washington, D. C.,
May 14, 1887.*

C lara called a meeting of her entire investigative team, including Sarah Bernhardt, since all entertainment in the capitol had been curtailed after President Cleveland instituted martial law. This was the only federal implementation of such measures since Abraham Lincoln did it at the outset of the Civil War in July, 1861. Many in congress and in the press were calling it an "egotistical, overreaching measure, not worthy of the Executive Office."

This time, she was prepared for such a meeting. She did her legal research, and she ordered food. The smorgasbord of sandwich accoutrements and snacks was beside the large, circular conference table in the center of the suite, and two waiters ran amongst the investigators, including the two Secret Service men from the Treasury Department, pouring tea and coffee and asking if anybody needed anything. She made certain the telephone table was within Dr. McFarland's reach from his seat at the table.

Around her, seated to her right, were Captain Isaiah Lees, Laura de Force Gordon, Sarah Bernhardt, Detective Hubert Abercrombie, and journalist and former congressman, Henry Watterson. As there were several legal minds at the table, she wanted to first discuss martial law being imposed in Washington.

"As we know, Lincoln was the only president to institute federal martial law in all of the states. President Cleveland's mandate, on the other hand, is limited to the District of Columbia. I am assuming that the local police know some of the same facts that we now know. According to Laura, we have also been placed under suspicion until the kidnappers call. Therefore, until that happens, we must curtail our private investigation."

Laura frowned.

"I disagree. Since the president was unable to convince congress to suspend the writ of habeas corpus, we are free to investigate, until and unless a court issues a warrant for our arrest."

Isaiah nodded.

"Laura is correct. I read in the early morning's *Post* that there are already three law suits against the Executive branch, challenging his use of militia to sweep the city. They are using the 1878 Posse Comitatus Act as their basis to argue, since it forbids the use of the military in domestic law enforcement."

She had read that same article.

"Cleveland, I am certain, will argue that Maryland and Virginia's governors voluntarily contributed militia members to assist in the search, and no federal army troops were involved. I want to pursue two important areas of discussion aimed at finding my son and the First Lady. One is the possible existence of a religious or other cult in these matters. The other is the criminal gang theory developed by Mr. Watterson."

She opened a large library book she had obtained yesterday, at the suggestion of Dr. McFarland, from the Library of Congress, after she learned about the tattoos on the bodies of the three dead women.

"President Cleveland and his men may be working on this theory, since our kidnappers may, in fact, be a group of fanatics. Martial Law was previously declared in Illinois and Utah, when the two leaders of the Mormon religious group, Joseph Smith and Brigham Young, violated the laws of the United States."

Laura raised her hand.

"Yes, I remember that because their religion violated the freedoms we hold so dear in our suffrage movement. In Illinois, the state of Missouri tried to extradite the Mormon founder, Smith, for the attempted assassination of Missouri's governor. Smith, who was mayor of a small town in Illinois called Nauvoo, had his town's lawyers draft a writ of habeas corpus to free him, and prevent his extradition to Missouri. In the Utah case, Brigham Young and his followers practiced both polygamy and slavery, and the Federal Government wanted to stop him because both practices violated our Constitution, and it led to a militant confrontation. Some even called it a war."

She held up the drawing of the lion-headed, winged, and nude man-god.

"Speaking of religious symbols, this image was tattooed on the backs of all three dead women in this case. Eloise Strong, Erin Scully, and Mrs. Caroline Taylor."

The Divine Sarah, who was wearing the blue stage uniform of the Paris gendarmes, pointed at the book.

"How fascinating! It must obviously be a symbol of male dominance. The way the Roman Emperor, Caligula, marked his harem of men and women."

Dr. McFarland chuckled.

"Quite appropriate, Sarah. In Greek and Roman antiquity, the tale of Hercules, or Heracles, to the Greeks, and his twelve labors, involved the hero's rescue of women held captive in the Nemean Lion's cave. This lion was impervious to weaponry, and the lion lured warriors to his cave by keeping these women hostage."

She noted that Sarah was obviously intrigued. "Thus, Hercules broke the lion's back to save the women. But why would this particular tattoo be on women who were killed?"

Dr. McFarland smiled.

"This statue of the lion-headed and snake-encircled man was found inside a Mithraeum, which was the place where Roman male members of this cult performed ritual initiation rites during the first through fourth centuries. The main feast was held on December 25th, the same day as our Christmas. Mithra was a god invented by ancient Persians and Indian Aryans, who were in competition with the Christian Jesus. These pagan worshipers of Mithras, a sun god, were eventually slaughtered out of existence by the rival Christians. The Jesus story was also about a sun god, complete with the nature symbols in the Garden of Gethsemane, at the Last Supper, and during the sacrifice on Golgotha. In fact, it's quite similar to the way we rationalize the massacre and captivity of the Native followers of so-called pagan religions in this country."

She decided to intercede with the connection to the present case.

"In typical male aggrandizement, Mithras was born from a

rock, and his name is derived from the Persian and Sanskrit 'mitra,' meaning a contract, agreement or covenant. These male members greeted each other with a secret handshake, for which we today recognize in legal terms as the gentleman's way of concluding an agreed-upon negotiation or treaty."

Laura scowled.

"Quite misogynist, as usual."

Dr. McFarland laughed.

"Indeed. These places of worship were easily created for most any location or human activity. During battles, inside a fortress or city, or even beneath the churches and temples of other religions. All that was required was a room with a table for dining and an altar where the sacrifice of a bull could be replicated, literally or symbolically, by the highest leader in the cult, called a Pater, or father."

She noted that the mention of a sacrificial element caught Isaiah's attention.

"Hercules could kill the lion, and Mithras could kill the bull. What was their goal in performing these acts?"

"Captain, good question. I shall ask you a question. What is the goal of the Christian Mass?"

"To remember the sacrifice that Jesus made to redeem mankind of its sins?"

"Allegedly. And since Mithras was a competing religion to early Christianity, it also had the goal of redemption for those who participated in the secret mysteries. Unlike Christianity, however, there was no central hierarchy of sages or religious texts created. Only the ritual of the slaying of the bull, accompanied by a feast and the iconography to represent the other, more natural symbolism of redemption and purification. There were also different levels or grades of membership."

"Purification?" Detective Abercrombie smirked. "On my daddy's farm, there was nothing pure happening when we slaughtered a bull for meat. Just a whole lot of blood."

"Again, like Jesus, Mithras was a sun god. However, unlike the Christian myth, in which Jesus must be sacrificed to free the spirit of man into eternal life, Mithras sacrifices a bull, which is then eaten together with the sun god in a pagan feast. In the iconography, a woman, represented by the moon, is also included. There were probably women used during their feasts, one would imagine, for one purpose or another."

Dr. McFarland again chuckled.

Detective Abercrombie was very interested, she realized. "Are you going to tell the president and his police about this?"

She decided to admit her bias to the group.

"No, not until we get the call from these kidnappers. We may not tell them then, unless it's meaningful to the situation. I am not even certain this means anything at this juncture. Which brings me to the second thread of our possible inquiry. Mr. Watterson, would you mind paraphrasing your gangland theory of our perpetrators?"

She saw that he was between bites of a quite large roast beef sandwich. Just before he could swallow it down with a glass of milk, the telephone rang. Dr. McFarland picked it up. The two Secret Service men nodded at him, and he nodded back at them.

"Hello? No, but I am her legal representative. What is it you want?"

She watched the doctor's face. His gray eyebrows furrowed in concentration, and he nodded twice in agreement with whatever was being said to him.

"Yes, I understand. However, I cannot negotiate with you until we know the exact details of how the money shall be delivered and how you might deliver our loved ones to us."

The doctor listened intently for five minutes.

"May I confer with his mother and with the president's representatives? It should not take too long."

He looked over at her and then at the two Secret Service men. He set the telephone down on the table and motioned for her and the two men to follow him over to the couch on the other side of the room.

She followed them and walked up to the doctor.

"What did they say?"

She touched Dr. McFarland's arm.

His eyes stared over her shoulder and had a distant quality to them.

"I know the amount of money they require for the release of the First Lady. They want Tiger's Eye gems worth one hundred thousand dollars."

"Does that include the amount for David?"

She wondered why he had left her son's name out of the statement.

"I am sorry, Clara. The spokesman said he cannot negotiate for the release of David at this point in time. They want to be certain all goes well."

"I don't understand. If they receive their money, then how important can my son ultimately be to them?"

She felt the wave of emotion fill her chest and constrict her throat. "I shall not allow it!"

The older of the two Secret Service men spoke. His eyes were gray, together with the streaks of gray in his beard, and his formal dark blue suit gave him the appearance of a senior accountant.

"Mrs. Foltz, we can secretly mark the Tiger's Eyes with indelible etchings. When they attempt to exchange them, the jeweler or other merchant will be able to immediately notify us of the bearer's identity. We shall track their location and release David with no harm done."

She was not convinced.

"Did he sound like the illiterate and bigoted person who wrote the note found in Mrs. Cleveland's chauffer's jacket?"

"Yes, he did have a deep Southern drawl. He also, at one point, mentioned the First Lady being a nigger-lover."

Dr. McFarland was uncomfortable saying the words. She felt resigned about what she knew she must do.

"I want to finish my conference discussion. How are they supposed to get the Tiger's Eye gems delivered to them?"

Dr. McFarland looked at the senior Secret Service agent.

"They stipulated only one person can deliver the Tiger's Eye gems. If they see any other suspicious people around this person, as he makes the delivery, they will shoot him and kill both the First Lady and David."

"One person. Were they more specific?" The agent said.

"Yes. Metropolitan Police Detective Hubert Abercrombie shall deliver the Tiger's Eye gems to the location. He is to be in this hotel room tomorrow morning at ten. A call will be made informing him of the location to take the ransom gems. They will also put the First Lady and David Milton on the telephone to verify their good health. Once they have the gems, they will release Frances Cleveland at an unspecified location. She will be safe." Dr. McFarland looked directly at her. "This is most interesting. They claim to be a large organization, which has many members inside the Cleveland Administration. If they hear that any plan has been made to rescue David, before they give the word, he will be immediately executed."

She felt her heart throbbing in her throat, and she almost gagged.

"Doctor. Please. I want to finish our meeting."

"Very well. One more thing. They will call us again to tell us where they left the First Lady."

The younger Secret Service man was taking notes.

She completed her meeting with her team by first explaining the ransom demands. Detective Abercrombie made a comment about these gangsters enjoying the prospect of killing a Negro cop. Mr. Watterson then explained the theory he had about this group being headed by the Trenton gang leader Dante Cross. He also thought the tattoos on the women could be something the criminal element would use to mark its possessions.

"Detective Abercrombie has already questioned baseball player, Fleet Walker. Walker admitted to meeting with Cross, and I think it would be best that we call to see if Cross is there, or if he might be in Washington right now."

Watterson looked at his friend, the detective. "In fact, I think you should bring Walker into the station for further questioning before tomorrow morning. If he's part of this conspiracy, then he might tip his hand."

"Good point." Isaiah looked enthused, she noticed. "I have been able to trap many criminals that way in San Francisco."

"*Mai oui! Monsieur*, I would love to ask him some questions about this case. May I?"

Sarah Bernhardt was interested in the case as well.

"Certainly, Miss Bernhardt. You may come with us to the D. C. Jail after this meeting is over."

Detective Abercrombie smiled at the actress.

"Clara, we will be with you tomorrow. Don't be frightened."

Laura reached across Captain Lees and grabbed her hand.

"Thank you," she said. "Detective, you can bring Walker in for questioning, Mr. Watterson can contact Dante Cross, and I shall work with Dr. McFarland about ascertaining information concerning the tattoos on the three women. I still believe it may be key to our understanding these kidnappers and their motives."

She arose from the table, as did the others. Abercrombie and Watterson left with Sarah Bernhardt.

Laura remained at the table with Dr. McFarland and Isaiah. She again opened the book about the cult of Mithras and stared down at the complicated symbols on the page. In her mind, she saw David Milton being held down upon a granite tabernacle, inside a dark cave, and a red-hot branding iron was being lowered onto his tender white back. The image of the flying lion snake man was stamped in blood and black ink, as he screamed for his father, Jerimiah, and not her.

***

The White House, 1600 Pennsylvania Avenue. West Wing, Oval Office.

Grover had been drinking. He signed the two hundredth veto of what he called "fraudulent pension bills" that morning and started on the Scotch after lunch. Colonel Lamont kept filling his glass from his personal bottle in the Oval Office desk drawer. His life without Frankie was unbearable. All he could picture was her lifeless but lovely form, nude and ravaged, inside some disheveled hideout, the kidnappers leering down at her.

The D. C. Commissioner, Bill Webb, was standing in front of a map of the city, pointing to the location of the Hotel Willard down the street. Grover thought the former police superintendent looked rather dashing in his black suit, and he always enjoyed drinking with "Wild Bill," as he called him whenever they were both in their cups. He envied his wavy-brown hair, streaked with gray. His muscular physique, and his deep bass, authoritative voice, had made him the best candidate for President of the Board of Commissioners.

"The call stated that Detective Hubert Abercrombie was to deliver the Tiger's Eye gems to a location they shall specify tomorrow morning. We believe they know about the detective because he is in charge of the jail where Eloise Strong was held. His name was in all the newspapers. We were able to get the gems from a dealer at the British Embassy."

"Where are they found?" Augie said.

"He gets them from their colony in Australia. They are six dollars per carat."

Webb picked up a piece of chalk and wrote the formula on the blackboard next to the map.

"There are 2,267 carats to a pound. 2,267x6 (each carat) is 13,602 per pound. 100,000÷13,602= 7.35 pounds. They will each be marked so that a jeweler can see, through magnification, the specific insignia."

Grover had difficulty focusing on Webb's body. He seemed to be waving like a stalk of corn in the wind. He sat down in his leather armchair. He was happy to have Augie there to respond to the more complex planning.

"The president will want all care to be taken to preserve the life of Mrs. Cleveland. What makes you believe they will release her?"

Augie walked over to the map and pointed to the Murder Bay section of the city.

"If they release her here, she might be immediately kidnapped once more."

"The kidnappers have said, once they receive the gems, they will call the hotel again with the location where they left Mrs. Cleveland."

Grover leaned back in his chair.

"What about that kid? The attorney's boy. If they harm him, my re-election chances may become jeopardized."

"It is a risk we must take, Mr. President. They have promised to release him once the transfer is made. These are criminal types who understand we will eventually uncover their lair. They want to retreat as soon as possible." The commissioner again pointed to the map. "We can have thousands of men swarming the area as soon as we discover a vicinity where they might be."

Grover stood up, weaving slightly in place.

"I understand. We must have Frankie returned. The American people have been sending me thousands of letters and postcards. Her face is in every tavern, home, and store in the District. As soon as she is released, she shall be brought to me immediately. Is that clear?"

Both men turned toward him.

"Yes sir. Quite clear."

***

D. C. Central Detention Facility, 1901 D Street, Southeast, Washington D. C.

The scarred detective, Abercrombie, brought Moses in for questioning. The policeman guaranteed he was not under arrest and that they were close to capturing the kidnappers of Frances Cleveland and David Foltz. He was going to be questioned to determine all he knew about the gang leader Dante Cross.

The room he was in was pitch dark, and he could not see any details around him. He could hear movement around his chair, and he could smell the odor from a cigar, and the perfume of a woman, but he had no knowledge of where Abercrombie was. He had not been treated this way by any police, even when he was hauled in for drunk and disorderly on the road with a baseball team.

"I will now turn on a light. It will be cast directly into your face, and I do so to keep you honest."

The disembodied voice sounded like that of the detective, but he couldn't be certain. The spotlight bathed his head in light. The glare made him squint and see spots. The voice became a phantasm, a haunted refrain.

"Were you aware that the Department of the Treasury now has electronic illumination at night? It is true. With that illumination, it seems, there has been another problem to arise. At the same time, a species of spider has discovered that game is plentiful in that vicinity, and that it can ply its craft both day and night. In consequence, their webs are so thick and numerous that portions of the architectural ornamentation are no longer visible, and when torn down by the wind, or when they fall from decay, the refuse gives a dingy and dirty appearance to everything with which it comes in contact. Not only this, but these arachnoid adventurers take possession of the portion of the ceiling of any room which receives the illumination."

"Are you insane? What are you doing to me?"

He tried to stand but realized there were clamps around his legs keeping him in the chair. He waved his arms in a futile attempt to find the speaker.

"Are you one of these spiders, Mr. Walker?"

He could tell this was another, much different voice. It sounded more feminine, with a liltingly soft accent.

"What do you mean? Stop speaking in riddles. I thought I was being questioned about Dante Cross."

He decided to tell them all he knew about Cross, but now he was afraid of what was happening. Did the scarred Negro have the white demons with him to break his will?

"I called Trenton, and Mr. Cross is not there. He is right here in Washington. Are you both prepared to retrieve the ransom for Mrs. Frances Cleveland? Where is Cross now? When are you supposed to meet him?"

"I don't know about any kidnapping. Dante Cross gambled on sports, yes. He tried to get me to shave runs in the games I played, but I told him I would never jeopardize my status as a professional ball player. I *was* telling you the truth. I met him three times, dammit, and that was all."

"I am not so certain, Mr. Walker. If you *are* telling the truth, then you won't be meeting with Mr. Cross later tonight or in the morning. If we discover you have informed him of our interest in this case, you will be arrested and jailed. Am I making myself clear?"

Panic filled him with the dread he had always felt concerning the white world around him. The demons were circling, and he knew he must hide somewhere until all of this was over.

"Yes. Very clear. You need not worry about me. I will lock myself up when I return, and you will not see me on the streets or anywhere else."

The words came out of his mouth in one breath.

The light was extinguished, and it was dark again. He could hear steps going away from him. Someone else released the clamps on his legs, grabbed his shoulders, and pulled him up. This person wrapped a blindfold around his eyes, and a cloth was tied around his wrists behind his back.

Two hands grabbed him by both arms and pushed him out of the room. He could hear the sound of crickets, smell the damp night, and he felt the steps he took turn from wood, to concrete, and then to gravel.

"I am putting you inside this buggy, and my driver will take you back to Howard University. He will then remove your blindfold and untie your hands. If you leave your room, you will be followed. If you meet with Dante Cross, you will both be arrested."

As he sat inside the buggy, he could feel the white spiders moving around inside the carriage with him, weaving their webs upon his face, his arms, and his ankles. Attempting to sink their fangs into his light brown skin, trying to poison him with their bigot venom.

Later, as he sat on the chair beside the card table, he watched a spider in the ceiling corner of his room. He realized they were correct. Spiders waited until their prey came to them. If light drew their victims in, so much the better. At that moment, he knew. He had to find the spiders' webs before the white demons escaped.

Chapter 9: Spiders' Webs

Willard Hotel, 1401 Pennsylvania Ave. NW, Washington, D. C.,
May 15, 1887, 9:45 AM.

The telephone was on the small table in the center of the hotel suite. Surrounding it, seated in a concentric, ever-widening circle, were the people appointed by the President of the United States to protect and to retrieve his twenty-one-year-old wife and, coincidentally, Clara's teenaged son.

She knew it was doubly worrisome because May 15 was David Milton's sixteenth birthday. She understood his sensitive ways, and the prospect of his being kept prisoner by gangsters, or other criminal outlaws, was making her panic inside, as she realized her time to solve this case was dwindling steadily.

In addition, once the authorities retrieved the First Lady, they would soon forget about her son. It was up to her and her group to find him, and she was going to achieve her goal to the best of her abilities.

She was so focused on finding him that she could not tell her family in San Francisco what had happened. Money from Mrs. Mary Hopkins arrived, so there were, thankfully, no money problems, but she could not answer the birthday greetings and telegrams from her family back home.

She saw that the Secret Service had placed Detective Abercrombie next to the telephone because he was responsible for the delivery of the ransom gems. All members of her team were briefed as to what would happen, but she knew that life was not as straightforward as our plans. Any number of unforeseen circumstances could occur to cause a disastrous result. Isaiah taught her well, however, and she knew the only way to succeed in the pursuit of the hunted was to understand their motives and their methods.

She was seated in the circle of chairs which contained her team: Dr. McFarland, Isaiah, Sarah, and Laura. Today would determine how they would pursue the case. Her compiled evidence pointed in one direction, but the present direction held the most promise. She actually hoped this was going to be the answer, but her intuition told her it could become something quite different.

The telephone rang. It was five minutes before the kidnappers were supposed to call.

Detective Abercrombie answered.

"Hello?"

She watched his face. He smiled.

"Thank you, Fitz. We can now assemble our theories. I must hang-up. I am awaiting a most important call."

Abercrombie looked directly at her.

"The medical examiner isolated the poison in the brains of the two women. It was a deadly liquid made from the Angel's Trumpet flower. I shall detail its toxicity and effects later."

Her mind became a colorful, Chinese revolving puzzle. Several images flashed from her memory and from her notes to click into place. The effect of this information was like an implosive sequence of insights, and her body felt as if it might levitate. She had a difficult time containing her urge to discuss these insights with Dr. McFarland at that very moment.

The telephone rang again. She could see it was exactly ten on the wall clock.

"This is he. Yes, I know that location. I understand. No, there won't be anybody but me. I shall tell them."

He looked at the receiver for a moment. He handed it to the older Secret Service agent.

"It's the First Lady."

"Hello? Mrs. Cleveland? This is Hiram Palmary. I am a member of the Treasury's Secret Service. What is the name you gave President Cleveland when you were a child? What is the birthdate of your deceased father? Very well. I am happy to hear you are in good spirits and health. We shall have you back soon. Yes. I will do that." She watched Palmary thrust the telephone at her. "It's your son, David Milton. He wants to talk to you."

She took it and held it to her ear. She whispered into the

mouthpiece, as if it were going to bite her.

"David? This is your mother."

She could tell by his voice it was he. He told her that they gave him a small birthday celebration, and he even blew out candles on a cake. He had to do it blindfolded, so he needed to take their word that he blew the candles out to get his wish.

"Have they harmed you in any way, David?"

He told her he was treated very well. "In fact," he whispered, "Father is here."

When David told her that Jerimiah was with him, she believed the boy was experiencing mental hysteria, like the women she met in the Stockton State Insane Asylum.

"How do you know? You can't see him."

He explained that the kidnappers brought him there from San Jose, and he was now a member of their group. David said his father told him they were special people, and they were working for a good cause. She tried to assimilate all the information she collected about the case in her mind at once, to see how this new piece could fit. She would need to discuss it with her team.

She wished her son a happy birthday in a voice that was as calm and motherly as she could enunciate. David told her his father said he would see her soon if all went well.

She placed the telephone back into its cradle. She knew she could not tell the police about Jerimiah. In fact, she did not even know if he was there.

The two Secret Service men walked over to Abercrombie, and Agent Palmary spoke.

"Do you have the route?"

Abercrombie nodded.

"Yes, but I have never read about or experienced a money drop like this before. I must proceed to the Potomac Aqueduct Bridge in Georgetown. You must station roadblocks to prevent all traffic from both sides of the bridge."

"I shall inform the White House. We can get look-outs stationed with binoculars inside the warehouses and on a few barges."

Agent Palmary made notes.

"I am to go exactly fifty-five yards on the bridge toward Rosslyn, Virginia. At that point, when it is exactly noon, I am to drop the gems over the starboard side of the bridge, with all of the gems stored inside a small, water-proof safe."

She saw that Isaiah could not contain his incredulity.

"It will sink to the bottom! How do you suppose they'll get it from there?"

"I must leave the bridge immediately. If they see anybody on the bridge for the next two hours, they will immediately kill the First Lady and young David Foltz. After three hours, at exactly three in the afternoon, they will release Frances Cleveland at an undisclosed location within the District."

"It can't be in a crime-ridden section." The Secret Service officer pointed out.

"Correct. They know that. She will be in an area that is safe."

Abercrombie stood up.

"Mr. Watterson, would you assist me with loading the safe on the carriage? It's parked outside the hotel."

Watterson also stood.

"Certainly."

Abercrombie smiled.

"Gentlemen and ladies. I shall now be on my way. May fortune be with me, and may we soon see our First Lady back in the White House and, soon after, the young lad, David Milton, back in the loving arms of his family."

***

Meridian Hill, N.W., Washington, D. C., May 15, 1887, 3:30 PM.

Moses Walker was there waiting at Meridian Hill. He remembered what Eloise Strong told him at the jail after she said she was again a slave. She told him to go to Meridian Hill to find the answer. He knew this was the magic center of the white demons' world.

It all became clear to him after he was questioned by the

105

disembodied voices inside the jail. The white demons controlled everything, and the answer as to how they were going to keep slavery going could be found at Meridian Hill.

An hour before, he stood beside the Jefferson Pier stone, which memorialized the location for the establishment of slavery throughout the land, in 1804. The land was too unstable to construct the true memorial, which was now 391 feet northwest from where he stood. The other Virginia slave master, George Washington, had his monument completed in 1885, and he visited it first, while he played baseball in the Washington D. C. of 1886.

A white obelisk, modeled after the original biblical slave-holders, the Egyptians, it stood 554 feet 7 $^{11}/_{32}$ inches tall, according the National Park Service plaque at its base. At the top, to protect it from God's lightning bolts, was an aluminum apex, a metal worth more than silver when it was installed.

The Washington Slave Monument was the tallest structure in the world today. Why should it not be so? The return of the masters, the white demons, was going to happen, and he was waiting for that moment to begin. Would they arise from the earth all around him, like the walking dead, to re-take the cities and towns, and ply their official duties? Were they waiting inside that freak of a white monument? What was going to be the signal for them to pour forth and re-take the land?

But Eloise Strong told him to go to Meridian Hill. That was where the Meridian Stone was. He had to walk two miles, and he had done so.

Now, as he waited, he could smell the spring flowers, hear the animals chasing and singing out for love in bloom. He wished his wife Bella could be there to see it all begin. Then, it would not be so difficult explaining it all to her.

As he looked back at it all, his first inkling came while on the road playing ball. The taunts from the benches and the stands came from the mouths of the white demons. They needed to gain more power, and so they did, and the monument built to that power, the diamond where he played, slowly swelled with pus and cancer. He could see it in his dreams at night, alone in his Negro room, at the Negro boarding house.

The three white bags on that diamond were filled with the lumpy and evil sperm of these future white masters. And the home plate monument, first constructed of marble, and then of rubber. This was the white base of power that he, inadvertently, spent his entire career protecting. He protected the white power, and now it was coming to fruition, walking slowly toward him in the mid-day sun.

She was a vision of loveliness. A white woman, who was more beautiful than any woman he ever saw. Could she perhaps be a child born from the same line of white slave owners who once fathered his grandmother? No. She must be the Sybil who was foretelling the day of slavery's return. She was smiling at him. He knew he must ask her.

***

Willard Hotel, 1401 Pennsylvania Ave. NW, Washington, D. C., May 15, 1887, 4:30 PM.

Clara overheard the location where the kidnappers took Mrs. Cleveland when they called the hotel at 3:30 in the afternoon. The coincidence of it being Meridian Hill turned to a possible inevitability when three Virginia Militiamen reported to Agent Palmary that they retrieved Frances Cleveland and returned her to the president at the White House.

When the soldiers informed them they had also arrested a colored man by the name of Moses Walker, who was accompanying the First Lady, it was the information she needed to add to her puzzle. The apprehension of the baseball player was associated with the coroner's report about the poison in the brains of Eloise Strong and Erin Scully, but she wanted to ask Dr. McFarland first before she could make it official.

After learning about Jeremiah being part of the kidnappers' group, she sat down with Dr. McFarland, Isaiah, Sarah and Laura to go over what she put together in the way of possibilities concerning the identity of the criminals. When she knew that Moses became involved, she realized that the deaths of the three women might be connected to the overall plot as well.

She told the group she was going to plan her own investigation and search for her son. When the gems were dropped over the bridge in Georgetown, and Frances Cleveland was returned, she knew the police needed a scapegoat.

"They knew about Moses Walker wanting to protect Judge Owens' killer. They also knew Eloise Strong told him in the D. C. Jail that she felt she became a slave again."

She saw that Laura was intrigued.

"By 'they,' I assume you mean the police, correct?"

After nodding, she continued.

"Eloise told Walker he could find out the reason she was enslaved by going to Meridian Hill, so he went there. That's when he became the sacrificial offering."

"What connection have you made with the poison, Clara?" Dr. McFarland wanted to know.

"You said the women died from a lethal dose, but what about a less than lethal dose? How does that affect the brain?"

She wanted the pharmacological answer before giving her connection to Walker.

Dr. McFarland explained.

"The danger in this plant is with its compounds known chemically as tropane alkaloids. These cause intense side effects, including visual and auditory hallucinations, confusion, and paralysis of the smooth muscles."

"There. You see. I believe Mr. Walker was given a lesser amount of this drug, and we can prove it when we visit him in jail."

She stood up.

Sarah Bernhardt stood up with her. "I was with Detective Abercrombie and Mr. Watterson when they questioned Mr. Walker last evening. In fact, I also asked him a question. You don't believe they gave him the drug, do you?"

"They may not have given him the drug, but the kidnappers certainly wanted him at Meridian Hill. You already told us about how the police told him about spiders at the Treasury Department.

What better way to gain control than to plant a suggestion and then manipulate his brain with a proven hallucinogen?"

She watched Isaiah stand up with Dr. McFarland.

"If Dr. Andrew McFarland says it can be fatal in stronger doses, I believe him. Do you now suspect Abercrombie and Watterson? Is it your contention that the drug was being used to influence the women all along? This is similar to our case at the asylum, is it not? The doctors there administered peyote to the patients to manipulate them."

"And what about the tattoos and their relationship to Mithras?" Sarah wanted to know.

"I have a few questions for Moses Walker and Frances Cleveland before I can answer those questions. I also want to ask Attorney General Garland a few questions about veterans' programs. Laura, I want you to research that specific issue and have your evidence when I question Garland at two this afternoon."

Laura nodded.

"I will see you there, partner."

She moved toward the door, nodding at the Secret Service twins.

"If my former husband is with my son, then I want to know what lured him there."

She opened the entrance and stepped out into the hall, holding the door open for her friends.

As Isaiah walked through, he stopped.

"Clara, do you suspect Abercrombie and Watterson of arranging for the arrest of Moses Walker?"

She sighed.

"I really don't know at this point. I do believe the detective thinks Walker was involved in the murder of the judge, and he knows some information about Walker that we don't know. I hope we can find out what that information is before it's too late."

***

Men's section of the D. C. Central Detention Facility, 1901 D Street, Southeast, Washington D. C., 6 PM.

"Don't let them poison me!"

Moses Walker was seated on the floor of his cell, his back cradled in the corner, his large right hand half-covering his face. He was peering at her through his fingers.

She discovered that Augustus Garland had formally arrested the baseball player for the murders of Eloise Strong, jail matron, Erin Scully, and Mrs. Caroline Taylor. Dr. McFarland was presently processing the papers needed to take a blood sample of Walker, and she was waiting for him. She also wanted him to interview the young man to see what mental state he was in.

Laura Gordon and Sarah Bernhardt were meeting her later, in the White House Blue Room, for a special meeting with Secretary Garland about her son and the questions she had about veterans' affairs. She believed she could possibly narrow her search for the kidnappers by doing so, but first she needed to see how Moses Walker fit into the ever-widening picture.

"Don't be afraid, Mr. Walker. I am here to help you. Did you go to Meridian Hill because of what Eloise Strong told you when you visited her?"

His eyes grew round and wide.

"Yes. She told me I could discover how slavery was taking over again. That's how I met the beautiful white woman. She told me the white demons held her prisoner, but now she is free. I helped her return home. Why did they put me in here? I saved the beautiful Sybil."

She walked over to him.

"Let me help you up, Mr. Walker. You need to sit on your cot where you can be more comfortable. You are Moses Fleetwood Walker, are you not?"

He took her hands, and she pulled on his arms until he was standing beside her. His torso under the blue dungaree shirt was muscular, although he was a thin man. He staggered over to the cot and sat on the edge near the pillow.

"I am Dante, and this is the Inferno. Where is Charon to escort us across the River Acheron? The white demons have arisen to begin their hell on Earth!"

She heard the jail door being opened, and when she turned around, Dr. McFarland was there, a syringe and needle in his right hand, and a wad of cotton in his other hand.

"Mr. Walker? My name is Dr. McFarland. I have permission to take a blood sample. I need to retrieve some blood from your arm in order to assess it for a possible illness you might have contracted."

He walked over to the cot, pulled a small chair over next to it, and sat down.

She watched the young man, as he gazed at the doctor and then at her.

"You are white. Are you demons come to enslave me?"

"No, my boy. We are here to protect you. If you are ill, then I can help to cure you as well. I am a physician."

Dr. McFarland smiled.

"Sybil said she would help me, but look where I am. If I give you my blood, you must promise me one thing." He looked up to the ceiling, and his brown eyes searched all around the cell.

"Of course. What is it?"

"Keep the spiders away. They have a venom that can enslave me."

Dr. McFarland reached out and took his right arm.

"I will do that. I shall first see if your blood has not been poisoned already."

These words seemed to soothe his troubled mind, and he allowed the doctor to insert the needle and draw his blood. She was curious about whether or not it contained any of the Angel's Trumpet poison.

"I will meet you back at the hotel. Please bring the results there."

She stood up.

"I will be there. I may spend a few more minutes with Mr. Walker, however. I want to assess his complete mental state."

He looked kindly over at Moses, and she saw the man's frightened expression turn calm, and then he nodded.

***

The White House, 1600 Pennsylvania Avenue. West Wing, Blue Room, 10:17 PM.

"We have our Metropolitan police officers searching this entire area where the First Lady was released. I promise you. We shall find young David soon."

Attorney General Augustus Hill Garland was standing before the city map that Commissioner Webb had used earlier that day. On the buggy ride over, Laura noted there were no longer militia soldiers searching the homes and buildings all over Washington. The crowds that came to the White House were yelling to see their "Frankie," but she was being questioned, at length, by officials in a back room.

She saw that Sarah Bernhardt was lounging in a leather chair, her legs tucked beneath her shapely body. She wore a green silk harem dress, complete with a transparent veil and cap. She was peering at the cabinet member as one would watch an actor who is auditioning for one her plays.

Laura decided to play one of her cards before Clara arrived. She had already done two hours of research into the present status of veterans and the president's methodical vetoing of most of the House bills that came to his desk asking for a pension.

"I see that the president can quickly call upon the military to help him find his wife, but he is very quick to refuse that same group when they request some regular pay after they become disabled during the discharge of their duties. Why is that, do you suppose, Mr. Garland?"

She watched him turn toward her, but he was unfazed by her rancor and sarcasm. He was a very short man, his Southern demeanor polite and well-mannered.

"As an attorney, Miss Gordon, I would assume you would have understood the problem of fraudulent appeals. The president did not, in fact, veto every pension bill. He approved those who complied with the Pension Bureau's rules, and he vetoed those who did not. It just so happens that there are more people from the Grand

Army of the Republic who have been promised pensions in exchange for a vote. The Republicans are very enterprising in that regard, as you may have noted."

She could now use her research to counter his argument.

"Quite understandable. However, how is that most of these approved pensions go to white men, and most of the monthly money goes to white men who are of a higher rank? One would assume both officer and enlisted to be in the same danger during wartime. In fact, the enlisted ranks were, more often than not, placed on the front lines of battles, were they not?"

He took three steps toward her and stopped. She noticed that his mustache twitched as he spoke.

"I can see your point, Miss Gordon. Although, as you should know, officers are more educated, and they are given leadership roles. This, to our president and to the bureau's good wisdom, means more to the country's stability."

"I see. But, what about this? No person—officer or enlisted—from the Southern militaries is given *any* federal assistance. They, who were trained in the same military academies and who had the same valor in their performance of duties, are not allowed to receive government help to stay alive in their state of complete mental and physical disability. What of their families? What of their new life in the union of these United States after conflict has ended?"

He took two more steps toward her, and she could tell his Southern charm was losing its luster. His voice was also losing its patient drawl.

"See here, good madam. The states must take care of them. That's the law in a republic."

"I see. The states. How about this? Are you aware of the statistics concerning how many pensions are given out and to whom they are given? At both the federal and state levels?"

She was coming in for the kill.

"I am aware, generally, of what the Bureau of Pensions does. The states are a different matter. We employ hundreds of official Examiners, who travel thousands of miles each year, to tend to the appeals of our veterans all over our great nation. Millions of dollars have been approved."

"Yes, well, I have looked at the official records, in my attorney's capacity, and I discovered that the least amount of money goes to women veterans and wives of combatants, Negroes, and Native Americans, who all, one might assume, served with honor or who are the spouses of military veterans who served with honor. Also, the downtrodden races of northern and southern Europe are left without pensions. As Shakespeare might remark, 'Can honor set to a leg? No. Or an arm? No. Or take away the grief of a wound? No. Honor hath no skill in surgery, then? No.' Why no monetary honor for these classes of honorable citizens, Secretary Garland?"

He stepped forward until he was standing directly in front of her. She could feel his hot breath, and his aspect was flushed.

"The president's commitment to our veterans is beyond reproach. But his commitment to ferret out fraudulent applications and the waste of the people's tax money on voting schemes are his main accomplishments. Are you, by any chance, a Republican, Miss Gordon?"

Clara entered the room, escorted by Colonel Lamont.

"Mrs. Clara Foltz, Esquire, sir."

She looked over at her partner and smiled.

"Now here is a staunch Republican. Wait one moment. Which party is today supporting a woman's right to vote?"

Garland sputtered, "I support any party platform that espouses national suffrage of women and their right to equal voting rights and equal justice in all things legal."

Clara walked over to her and placed an arm around her shoulder.

"You must be speaking about veterans' affairs already, Laura. Did you know my former husband, Jerimiah, is also a veteran of the Civil War, Mr. Garland?"

She noticed the attorney general was striking his leg with his right hand. The three women in the room outnumbered him, even though one was merely lounging in a chair.

Clara puffed out her chest.

114

"I have come to ask you some questions about why you arrested Mr. Moses Fleetwood Walker. I have reason to believe he may be innocent of any charges you may have against him."

Chapter 10: Where is Dante?

Willard Hotel, 1401 Pennsylvania Ave. NW, Washington, D. C., May 16, 1887, 8:00 AM.

After the late evening at the White House, Clara was happy to return to the hotel. She and Isaiah had a room together, and it was comforting to her to be able to lie in bed with him in the morning discussing what they knew thus far in their investigation.

She learned a lot from the others, especially Laura and Dr. McFarland, but it was her lover with whom she wished to confer her inner feelings about the possibility of her son being in danger, not to mention the chance that her former husband was involved with the conspirators.

As she twirled his gray chest hair around her fingers, she remembered that Jerimiah was the same age, fifty-seven. In fact, they had both served in the Union Army, but whereas Isaiah had not been physically or psychologically wounded, Jerimiah had been both. She wanted to talk to Isaiah about this, as she believed it had a lot to do with the present case.

She pulled herself up on the blue satin pillow and drummed on Isaiah's chest with her fingers. He was reading a Mark Twain novel, and she could see him grinning, something he rarely did during his daily rituals.

"I think the attorney general believed Detective Abercrombie's story about Moses Walker and the gang leader, Dante Cross. That is, until Dr. McFarland analyzed the ball player's blood and discovered he had been given a lesser dose of the Angel's Trumpet potion."

He turned toward her, placing his bookmark in place.

"Yes, my dear. You said McFarland was able to get the young man out of jail and into St. Elizabeths Hospital by using his mental analysis of the young man. Walker even invoked *The Divine Comedy's* Dante in his delirium."

"The doctor is a respected alienist. He testifies in court cases all around the country. Walker, he said, began to have an overly suspicious fixation about the white demons during his days on the road playing baseball."

He smiled.

"Yes, and the drug sent him over the edge into delusionary fantasies. I have seen that behavior before in the service. Men believe strange things under stress. I once had to convince a private to climb down from a tree because he thought he had reverted back into a primordial ape. It was his way of getting out of the war. We all have our methods of hiding from our fears, do we not?"

"That's my point. As soon as they released Mr. Walker, the White House immediately responded to Mr. Watterson's far-fetched ideas concerning the Redshirt bigots in town and the fact that Dante Cross was also capable of kidnapping and murder. Why do men always need something or someone to chase? Why can't they simply view the facts at hand before they connect the clues?"

"As Twain says, why do women always need five-dollar words when a fifty-cent word will do? You always say men are misogynist egotists, Clara. What do you call what you just said? They are the police. They want to find the kidnappers of your son. Searching down suspects is not a blind chase."

She was getting irritated, and she needed to get what she had been thinking about out into the open.

"They did not want to explore my avenue of investigation, however. Was it because I am a woman? I told them I thought there was a common denominator between the suspects, and I don't believe it's what the kidnappers want us to believe. My husband was a lot of things, but he was not an idiot or a bigot. Something lured him into the hands of those kidnappers other than simply telling him they had David Milton."

Isaiah touched her cheek with his hand.

"I understand. But you don't know what that lure was any more than they do. At least, they are tracking down possible witnesses who may have heard or seen why Jerimiah left San Jose to come here. His wife, his few friends. They aren't ignoring your idea completely."

"Yes, but it's rather obvious to me that the kidnappers purposely staged the kidnapping methodology. Excuse me for the five-dollar word. I don't believe they are necessarily bigots, gangsters, or mentally deranged fanatics. They could just be clever confidence tricksters. Most of my assembled clues, as a matter of fact, point to just that."

"All right. Get to your thesis. What do you suspect?"

She turned to face him so she could see if he smirked in any way after what she was about to tell him.

"I believe Jerimiah came to Washington because he was lured by some confidence game for veterans. Garland admitted that there were criminal examiners and fraudulent schemes, like the one concerning the slave pension. Tricking former slaves into believing the government would give them a monthly award. I think Jerimiah was tricked by a more intelligent ruse."

"Yes, but your son and the First Lady were kidnapped for ransom. Is this the activity of a mere confidence game? It seems more sinister, to me."

She touched his face with her hand.

"I love you, Isaiah. You always equalize me. Let's have some breakfast and get our group together again. We still need to interview the First Lady, and I want research done about confidence advertisements that may be out there."

He kissed the back of her wrist and pulled her on top of him. She shook her auburn hair and laughed, and they greeted each other in a much more intimate, five-dollar way.

***

"Good morning, everyone. As we now have a task ahead of us to interview the First Lady, Frances Cleveland, about what she experienced during the time she was kidnapped, I want to add another important job. We need to research all the newspapers in San Jose to see if there were advertisements concerning veterans earning pensions in Washington D. C. during the time frame in which Jerimiah might have left to come here."

All five of Clara's group were sitting around the conference table. There were no Secret Service twins, as the White House was no longer in charge of the telephone. They were, however, to report any calls from the kidnappers to the proper authorities.

"Since I already know the Library of Congress and its policies, I can do that for you."

Laura was seated directly across from her, with Dr. McFarland on her right and Sarah Bernhardt on her left. Isaiah was on Sarah's right side.

"Very well. Thank you, Laura. That will free me to visit Frances Cleveland at her Red Top farm in Georgetown Heights. The police have already debriefed her, but I have some questions they may not have asked."

She took out a sheet of paper from a folder on the table.

"I want to go over the facts we now know, and I wish to solicit your ideas about how we can proceed to answer the events that have occurred during the last week."

"Since the militia soldiers have returned to Maryland and Virginia, the only officers searching for David Milton are from the Metropolitan local police. Does anyone know how many there are at present?" Laura said.

"When I asked at the jail, they told me about twenty-five are presently searching," Dr. McFarland said.

"All right. That means our own investigation must be invigorated. Here are the facts we know. Detective Abercrombie delivered the valuable gems to the bridge in Georgetown, and he dropped the safe over the side at noon. Nobody reported seeing any water craft or persons on the Potomac to retrieve this safe. Any speculation as to how the kidnappers were able to retrieve these gems?"

Sarah raised her hand, and she nodded at her.

"Perhaps an underwater diver retrieved them? In France, we have such people who can dive for pearls inside oysters."

"Interesting, but somebody would have seen these divers go into the water." She pointed out.

"According to secret records after the war, there were over twenty submarines developed by both Union and Confederate governments. The *CSS Hunley* was the only one that sank a ship, but there must today be some kind of craft that can be used for such an underwater mission." Isaiah seemed enthused.

She nodded.

"That is excellent. We can assume the kidnappers had some kind of submersible craft to retrieve the safe of gems from the bottom. This leads one to believe these kidnappers already had some amount of wealth to afford such technology."

Laura raised her hand.

"They also had access to that infernal telephone. Which means they were probably in a location other than the poor sections of the District."

"However, they may have called from another location. If they chose to ask for Tiger's Eye gems, it would mean they had a method of selling these. That would also point to a more sophisticated, even international reach," Dr. McFarland said.

"Therefore, while we are narrowing in on a potential kidnapping group that is intelligent, wealthy, and sophisticated, the White House is searching for an illiterate, bigoted group, headed by an underworld lord named Dante Cross," Isaiah said.

She was enjoying how her group was coming around to her way of thinking.

"That is why my questions to the only person who has been with these kidnappers, Frances Cleveland, will concern all that we have been discussing. In addition, your search for a possible veterans' lure that would attract Jerimiah could conceivably get us closer to knowing who these culprits might be."

Sarah, unlike the other women in the group who wore conservative town dresses, was wearing a flamboyant dress of violet and red, with a peacock-feathered hat.

"Please, Mrs. Foltz. We must save young David. What else do you have on your list?"

She looked down at the sheet.

"Let's see. We now know the two women, Eloise Strong and her jail matron, Erin Scully, were poisoned with a hallucinogenic potion made from the Angel's Trumpet flower."

Sarah nodded. "Again, the choice of such a symbolically exotic poison speaks to your theory that they are very intelligent, no?"

"Correct. When I visited Mrs. Caroline Taylor's Home for Friendless Colored Girls, the same coroner who examined Strong and Scully was there to inspect the hanged body of Frances Cleveland's good friend. I had an idea the three deaths might be related, so I asked Dr. Fitzpatrick to call me with any results of his toxicology report on the body of Mrs. Taylor. He has yet to call me."

Dr. McFarland raised his bushy gray eyebrows.

"Therefore, if this drug were administered as a poison to all three, and as a hallucinogenic and weaker potion to Mr. Walker, then these same kidnappers may be behind it. Is that what you surmise?"

"It depends on the proximate cause of death of Mrs. Taylor. She may have been killed first and then hanged to make it appear to be suicide. Or, she might have been drugged the way Mr. Walker was drugged, and her confused and delusional state of mind may have caused her to commit suicide. Either way, yes, all three deaths were, most likely, related."

"And, all three women had the tattoo on their backs," Laura said.

"That brings me to my final point. When I mentioned the cult of Mithras, and then I remarked that I would not tell the White House about what we had discovered concerning this cult, I noticed that Detective Abercrombie was quite interested. In fact, he looked relieved. Why do you suppose he was interested?"

"I think he was just inquisitive. He is a detective, after all, Clara. Any abnormal group behaviors intrigue us. You should know that. I am frequently involved with the Tongs in Chinatown," Isaiah said.

"Yes. Possibly. But I believe he may know more about that cult than he lets on. I plan to watch his activities, more carefully, in any case."

She stood up.

"Shall we adjourn to our appointed rounds? Dr. McFarland, could you please man the telephone while we are out?"

He nodded at her.

Her group stood up.

Again, she asked to hold hands and say a prayer for the safety of David and Jerimiah. They all did so, with quiet solemnity.

***

Oak View/Red Top, Corner of Macomb and 35th Streets, Georgetown Heights.

She rode out to the Cleveland hideaway with Isaiah in a rented carriage from the hotel. The springtime weather was luxurious, and the odors of blooming wildflowers filled her with hope. If only they might discover the final clues to find David Milton, she could at last enjoy the season in all its presumed glory.

Laura and Sarah were going to do the research at the Library of Congress for the veterans' advertisements that might have lured Jerimiah Foltz to Washington. She mentioned to Isaiah that her women contacts with the Suffrage Movement returned home after Eloise Strong was found dead. It was now a criminal case rather than a murder trial to prevent the Capital Punishment of a suffragette.

"Look. There it is. Up ahead."

Isaiah pointed across her lap, out the carriage window, to a large, red-tiled structure that wore Victorian turrets on the roof like party hats, and the inviting porches gave it a summer look.

"I don't know. It seems different than our Victorians in San Francisco. Why is that?"

Isaiah grunted.

"I read that when Cleveland bought the place, it was just a farmhouse. He hired an architect named Poindexter to add the Victorian touches."

She craned her neck out the window to get a better look.

"It's almost ten, so she should be expecting us. The president, I was told, will be at the White House making the arrangements for their goodwill tour down South. There are several armed men on the grounds, I see, so he is also protecting the most popular ingredient of his tour."

"Yes. The *Post* remarked that security will be increased on that tour, as a result of this kidnapping."

She watched Isaiah open the door, step down, and reach out to take her hands.

"He wants to protect what he possesses, but he leaves the pursuit and capture of the guilty parties, and the retrieval of my son, to others."

She slid her bustle over the seat cushions and stepped onto the first wrung of the carriage ladder. Her decision to wear her ruffled orange taffeta spring dress, with matching straw hat, medium bustle, and parasol, met with Isaiah's approval. She remembered that it had also met with David Milton's approval, for different reasons, of course.

"You look very fetching, my dear," he said, and he gave her a peck on the cheek.

A pleasant thrill ran through her, as she remembered their early-morning tryst. She felt guilty, however, as her son was still missing.

She saw Frances Cleveland come bounding toward them from the porch, with the two Secret Service twins from the hotel leaping after her. She wore one of the dresses with an open neck, which the ladies from the Christian Temperance Union found so shocking.

"Mrs. Foltz! Welcome to Oak View. I thought we might talk on the veranda. It's so glorious outside, is it not?"

She took her hands, and she could see why the young woman was so popular in the press and with the American people. Her eyes were a deep, Caribbean blue, and her hair was a weave of gleaming black, with the stylish cut at the back of her neck that all the young women were imitating in their own coiffures.

"Mr. Lees, I see you come armed," Frances remarked, pointing at the .45 at his belt. "We have so many armaments around here, they might have better served poor General Custer at Little Big Horn than to protect one small woman such as I."

She laughed, and guided them over to the two wicker chairs on the front porch.

There were three filled glasses of iced tea, with mint and lemon, and a silver serving tray of various cookies. She thanked the older Secret Service officer, named Palmary, who pulled a chair out for her. The president was, quite obviously, not going to allow their conversation with his Frances go unattended.

"First of all, let me say that I am so sorry about your son. The kidnappers kept us apart during our stay, so I never had the pleasure of hearing from him." Frances took a sip from the tea and leaned forward. "They kept me blindfolded, with my hands tied behind my back. I would assume they did the same to your boy elsewhere in our prison."

"Do you recall what you overheard, Mrs. Cleveland? We believe they might have kept you both in the same building, even though not in the same room. Also, what did your other three senses tell you? Did you smell anything? Did they touch you with anything? Any special foods or drinks that you can remember?"

She could hear the First Lady's audible sigh.

"I knew you would ask me. I shall tell you exactly what I told the other policemen. The only normal consciousness I had took place on the first day I was taken to their facility, whatever that might have been. Beginning the next day, May 13, I believe it was, I began to have thoughts of an amazing variety of sensory perceptions. I could not distinguish odors from sounds, and I confused my memories with what I could touch in the present."

"I see. Do you believe they drugged you?"

Clara was immediately thinking about Moses Walker and his experience, as well as the three dead women.

"Yes, I do. The Surgeon General, John Hamilton, told me I was merely under stress. He said women often get hysterical when faced with the kind of inhuman pressures I was under." Frances looked at her as if she were addressing her mother. "He sounded exactly like my husband. I *know* I was drugged by those rapscallions!"

"I completely understand. My alienist friend and expert physician, Dr. Andrew McFarland, analyzed the blood of Mr. Moses Walker, the gentleman who found you on Meridian Hill. He was, most certainly, under the influence of a drug made from the Angel's Trumpet flower." She reached over and took hold of the younger woman's alabaster hands. "On another note, when you visited my former client, Miss Strong, did you meet a military veteran outside the jail before you entered?"

She saw a flicker of recognition in her pretty face.

"Yes, I did. I bought the Peruvian liquor from him to give to Miss Strong. I knew it! You're saying that liquor was poisoned. And Mr. Walker. He seemed as muddled and confused as I was. It was rather like the blind leading the blind. When I came to my senses, I told them that Mr. Walker had nothing to do with my condition, but they did not believe me. They arrested him immediately and hauled him off to jail, under my most fervent protestations."

She wanted to get to the heart of her inquiry, now that the proverbial "cat was out of the bag."

"We are doing our own investigation to find my son, and we most certainly know that all three of the female victims have been drugged by the same Angel's Trumpet potion as you and Mr. Walker. However, during that first day in captivity, what exactly did you overhear from these kidnappers? I don't care how strange or inappropriate it might have sounded. What did they say?"

She squeezed the First Lady's hands and smiled at her.

"The police have everything I heard on that first day, and that's why they believe the theory of Detective Abercrombie and Mr. Watterson. They told me that the names I heard, and the vindictive language the kidnappers used, were all part and parcel of this new anti-Reconstruction movement going on throughout the former Confederate states today."

Isaiah frowned.

"I'm afraid your husband has also continued the problem when he approved the Chinese Exclusion Act. What names did you hear them mention? Did they threaten anybody?"

Frances nodded.

"My husband and I greatly differ on immigration and civil rights issues. In fact, one of the names I heard them mention, Miss Ida B. Wells, challenged the Supreme Court ruling that struck down the 1875 Civil Rights Act."

She nodded. "I read about her heroic case. She won $500 at a local court, but the railroad appealed to the Tennessee Supreme Court, and she lost the case based on the Supreme Court's ruling."

Frances smiled. "Miss Wells came to visit me this year, at one of my Sunday White House luncheons for women of all colors and working classes. She is an extremely intelligent young woman, a suffragette, who was forced to move from a first-class ladies' car to the men's smokers' car on the Chesapeake and Ohio Railroad. She believed she had a right as a teacher, taxpayer, and law-abiding citizen to sit with similar ladies out of harm's way. I agreed with her."

"In which context did the kidnappers mention her name?" Isaiah inquired.

"They said the Washington D. C. newspaper, *The Evening Star*, for which she wrote, was going to be torched to the ground, with her inside it, I am afraid."

"Did they give any reason why?" She asked.

"According to the kidnappers, she was writing articles protesting the Jim Crow laws and new state constitution rules being drafted in the South. They said they wanted 'to keep niggers out of office and separate them from their white superiors.' The other Negroes they mentioned were political office holders."

"Their lynchings and threats seem to be working. There were over 1,500 Negroes in office during Reconstruction. Today, I believe, there are only five left. With none in the Executive branch and none in the Senate."

She stood up.

"Mrs. Cleveland, I believe we have everything we need at this point. These kidnappers had Southern accents, am I correct at assuming that?"

Frances also rose, as did Isaiah.

"Yes. But only that first day. The other days, I'm afraid, I was hearing many different sounds and having internal confusion so that I could not make sense of much of anything around me."

"What kinds of sounds or smells, if you don't mind my

asking?" She said.

"One day, I heard the sound of some kind of animal, perhaps a lion. It was a roar or growl. On the next day, it was the tortured sound I had heard only once before in my life. I could also smell smoke and perfumed incense of some kind."

The First Lady frowned and looked down at her feet.

"Where were you before when you heard that second sound?" She said.

"I was attending a bull fight in Madrid, during the world tour Stephen sent me on to learn about the cultures in other lands. It was the sound the poor animal made as he is being punctured by the knives of those Spanish men they call the Picadors."

"Thank you, Mrs. Cleveland. You've been most gracious and helpful. We shall inform you when we can find my son. I hope we can write to each other. My friends and I are also suffragists, although our speed to gain the right to vote is perhaps a bit more impatient than your own at present."

She smiled and was encouraged when the First Lady returned the smile. "Please, Mrs. Foltz. Call me Frances."

On their ride back to the hotel, she knew her instincts were now correct. Frances Cleveland had been intoxicated by the same drug as Moses Walker and the three deceased women. She had also met a veteran outside the jail, perhaps the same one she had met outside Caroline Taylor's Home for Friendless Colored Girls. Frances was also under a state of hallucination for most of the time she was held captive. However, the two sounds she heard were not, according to her reasoning, the aberrant delusion of a hysterical woman, as the police must have believed.

She turned to face Isaiah. He was again reading from his Twain comedy, chuckling to himself.

"Mithras," she said.

He turned toward her, a smile still playing under his mustache. It irritated her.

"Yes, my dear?"

"The sounds of the lion and the bull. Do they mean anything to you?"

She wanted to get that smirk off his demeanor.

"No, but perhaps Dr. McFarland might make something of it?"

He kept smiling.

She struck his bicep with her fist. "You dolt! The lion-headed snake man. And the bull that is sacrificed on the altar inside the Mithraeum."

Still smiling, he replied, "Of course! Why didn't I think of that?"

For her, it was a long ride back to the hotel after that exchange. She did know that the entire first day's experience for Frances had been a ruse to lead the police away from the real perpetrators and kidnappers of the First Lady and her son, David Milton.

Chapter 11: Flair for the Dramatic

Willard Hotel, 1401 Pennsylvania Ave. NW, Washington, D. C.,
May 16, 1887, 2:00 PM.

L aura, who was rarely invigorated, burst through the hotel room door out of breath. Clara was sitting with Isaiah on the divan, going over the possible questions they might ask Detective Abercrombie and the journalist, Mr. Watterson.

"You will not believe what we discovered!" Laura erupted, waving her arms, running over to her, and sitting down by her side. Miss Bernhardt, she noticed, walked calmly over to a leather chair and curled, cat-like, into it, staring back at them through her mascara and curly-black bangs, as if she had just dined on two love birds.

"I often have difficulty seeing your side of most everything, I must admit," she told her partner, smiling, and grasping her hands. "What is your latest illumination, Laura?"

"At first, we both searched the newspapers of San Jose for advertisements concerning any veteran pensions. Especially those that displayed connections to our case or to Washington D. C."

Laura sneezed. She often saw the older woman do this whenever she got overly excited.

She once told her friend that as an only parent, she attempted to explain the female orgasmic experience to her then nine-year-old daughter, Trella Evelyn, by using a sneeze as a metaphor. Both her daughter and Laura, at different times, found that analogy quite humorous, and they immediately sneezed.

"We had little luck for over two hours, in that dusty and dreary place, and then we found a similar ad, in two different newspapers. It was a solicitation for those men who had been held captive at Andersonville Prison during the latter months of the Civil War. The return address and telephone number to call were both located in Washington."

Laura pulled a sheet of paper from her purse and held it out to read.

"And, I quote, 'Attention: Good Union warriors who were imprisoned at any point in time at the Andersonville, or Fort Sumter, Confederate Prison in Georgia. We have private philanthropists who wish to donate thousands of dollars to supplement the government pensions of men who can qualify. Please contact us at U. S. Postal Office Box 2315, Washington D. C., or telephone the Washington D. C. exchange operator and ask for extension 7583.' After we read this announcement, we at first thought your Jerimiah would never apply to such an offer."

"He might try to lie his way into their graces," she pointed out.

"Quite right, Clara. Exactly what I came to believe. As a result, we did some research into the veterans' records section located inside the Army Medical Museum, on the second floor. Lo and behold, Jerimiah Richard Foltz *was* taken captive at the Battle of Chickamauga, and he spent almost two months inside Andersonville, from February 18, 1864 until April 1, 1865. He did not have to lie. His record proved his qualification."

"My God! He never acknowledged to me or to anyone else that he had been held captive in that wretched place."

She now understood the chasm between Jerimiah and the family was built upon a very heinous and secret experience.

Isaiah pointed at the sheet of paper in Laura's hands.

"If all he had to do was apply in writing or by phone, then why would he need to come to Washington?"

"Good question. Sarah and I talked about that as well. We surmised that he may have been recruited by this organization to work for them. As a result, he was asked to come to Washington."

Sarah spoke from her armchair.

"I called the young nurse, Katherine Gadfry, who lives with Jerimiah in San Jose. She verified the fact that her husband told her he was going to visit Washington to meet with fellow veterans of the Chickamauga battle."

"He lied to her," she said.

Laura frowned.

"If Jerimiah wanted to keep it a secret, then what happened

inside Andersonville must have been, in some manner, embarrassing or possibly even worse."

"Is it your idea that this is the group behind the kidnappings? It seems you are headed in that logical direction," she reflected.

Laura smiled.

"It is. Now here is our plan. Sarah says she can dress as a middle-aged male Union veteran, and I can be his legal custodian. I have official records to prove internment inside Andersonville under the name of Arthur Knowles, Sergeant, 4th U. S. Cavalry, under Colonel Robert Minty. We shall telephone this number and attempt to meet them in person. At our meeting, we hope to convince these people that we are willing to work as recruiters for them, or in whatever other capacity they might need."

"What if that assistance requires you to be drugged and branded with a lion-headed, naked snake-man tattoo in the small of your backs?"

She wanted to get their attention concerning the possible dangers that might await them.

Sarah uncurled her legs from beneath her bottom and stood up. Her violet and red dress was pleated with blue ruffles down the middle, her shoulders were crimson puffs of glistening silk, and her pointed red-and-black satin hat made her look like a bird of prey. It was difficult to imagine her as a masculine version of any species.

"Not to worry, Mrs. Foltz. We shall give a most magnificent performance. I have researched what occurred inside that prison, and my story will bring tears to their eyes. In no time, *mon ami*, the location of this nest of vipers will be uncovered. Your son, our dear David, will then be freed."

"Thank you, Sarah. I find your generosity on my son's behalf a most unselfish and sacred act. Why is it you are willing to risk your life in this effort?"

She finally had the courage to ask the great actress what she wanted to know for some time.

"I, too, have a son. His name is Maurice. His father is a Belgian nobleman named Charles-Joseph Eugene Henry Georges Lamoral de Ligne. I have been pursued by many rich men and nobles, and they all need grand names to go with their grand titles. He was the only man I agreed to bed. Why? He had the largest collection and variety of animals in Europe, and I am quite the animal fancier!"

"David said you were wed to another man. A Greek actor named Aristides Damala," she said.

"Alas, poor Aristides succumbed to his addictions, and I had to leave him. During the Franco-Prussian War, I was able to hide my sorrow by serving my country. I became a nurse and turned my theater into a medical field hospital."

"Indeed. That is quite noble of you, Sarah," Laura said.

"When I heard about your appointment to defend Miss Strong, and this case, I immediately became very close to you in spirit. When I finally met your David, he was everything my son was not. Unlike Maurice, David Milton loves the theater and acting. So, now do you see why I want to help you rescue him?"

"Yes. It is very clear to me now. While you two attend to the acting, Detective Lees and I shall be inspecting the pension records where you uncovered the information concerning Jerimiah. I believe Detective Abercrombie and Henry Watterson may also have some secrets about which they haven't admitted."

"*Bonjour, mesdames et messieurs*! Remember. Life begets life. Energy begets energy. It is by spending oneself that one becomes rich!"

She watched the Divine Sarah prance toward the exit, little Laura Gordon racing after her.

***

The Army Medical Museum, 511 10th St. NW, Washington, D.C., 3:30 PM.

Just before leaving the Willard Hotel, Dr. McFarland got the call from the coroner, Dr. Fitzpatrick, about the toxicology analysis of Mrs. Caroline Taylor, the alleged suicide. He told Clara that she was not exposed to any of the Angel's Trumpet potion, but she did have a drug overdose that killed her. She died from a morphine

132

injection.

She looked up at Isaiah as they entered the Army Medical Museum.

"That explains how the group probably manipulated her and possibly even Eloise Strong. They were addicted to morphine and were dependent so much on the drug that they did anything this group told them."

He smiled down at her.

"It may also explain the exchange the two women had while Miss Strong was in jail. Scripture has often been used as a secret code for many imprisoned people. Do you suppose they were planning to expose this kidnapping group?"

He held the door for her, and she stepped into the foyer.

"Excellent insight, Isaiah. I can see why you're Captain of Detectives. It might also explain the tattoos, and perhaps even why Eloise killed Judge Owens."

He furrowed his owlish eyebrows.

"Why? Your insight goes much deeper than my own, my dear."

"What if the judge were against some legislation that was being proposed by congress? Legislation that might put an end to the business activities of our kidnappers. We have already said they are not illiterate hayseeds. They are, most likely, very intelligent and possibly even wealthy entrepreneurs."

Isaiah nodded and took out his badge and Army identification to show the clerk when they arrived on the second floor.

"I see. Therefore, Owens told Miss Strong he was against this proposed legislation and would probably declare it illegal when he became a member of the Supreme Court. When she told her handlers, the kidnappers, what she knew, they ordered her to kill the judge."

She stepped behind her beau onto the elevator. The Negro operator lifted them up to the second floor's Pension Records Section, and the doors opened.

***

Fourth White House, New Kent County, Virginia, 8 PM.

Although they had little time to rehearse, Sarah Bernhardt and Laura de Force Gordon devised a method whereby they believed they could rationalize any information they may not know. Laura, as the legal guardian and nurse, explained to the person on the telephone that Sergeant Knowles had been kicked in the head by his horse during the Chickamauga skirmish at Reed's Bridge. His memory was affected, and he had difficulty identifying people, places and dates.

Even with this qualification, the person on the line was not deterred. When he heard the veteran Knowles was in Washington, and was held prisoner in Andersonville, directions to the estate home in Virginia were immediately given to them.

Sarah was dressed by her talented costume and maquillage professionals at the National Theater. Laura, usually very skeptical about such matters, was convinced of her comrade's masculine presence.

To add to the disguise, Sarah was given a scar along the forehead, extending down her right cheek, to the end of her chin. She wore worker dungarees, a woolen lumberjack's plaid shirt, and red suspenders. Although she was a bit short, at five feet, she made up for her stature with male gestures and poses and short, curly-black hair that accompanied her bold, albeit tenor voice.

Laura chose to wear a nurse's uniform of blue, with a snow-white, frilled cap, long white stockings, and matronly black shoes. It was agreed that she would do most of the talking, until and unless questions were asked directly of Sarah.

Their hired hansom cab was taken from the train station in Richmond out to estate mansion in New Kent County. The train ride from Union Station in Washington had taken three hours, and the ride out to the given address another two hours.

When she saw the big sign in front of the lighted residence, Laura tried to recall where she had seen it before. It read "The Fourth White House is Producing New Cures for the World!" The house was standing on a few acres of land next to a river. It was two stories tall, with a six-column porch. By Civil War plantation standards, it was small.

When she knocked on the tall, Georgian mansion's door, she could hear scurrying within. The door swung open, and they were greeted by a tall smiling Negro butler who escorted them into the main drawing room.

"Dr. Lightfoot will be down shortly. Please wait for him in the library."

He pointed to a room off to the right, in which could be seen electric lights bathing rows of many books.

For the moment, however, they were both attracted to the assortment of posters and original art work hanging on the walls of the drawing room. She was instantly aware of the advertisements she had seen before under the name of Fourth White House.

One poster read "Cure Backache with FWH Smartweed & Belladonna Plasters." It had a colorful picture of two children building a little stick house beside a white picket fence. Another poster said, "Cure Your Nagging Cough and other Pains with FWH's Heroin Hydrochloride: for all ages." It depicted a man wearing a military uniform on crutches being given a teaspoon of the liquid from a pretty young nurse.

The largest poster of all said, "The Cure for All Addictions: Dr. Lightfoot's Out-of-Body Treatment: Order by mail for the home cure, or come to our week-long emancipation cure!" It showed two photos. The first of a decrepit-looking person with sagging posture, torn and dirty clothing, and he was looking up, as if to say, "Why me?" In the second photo, this man had been transformed into a vigorous soul wearing a bowler, a snappy tailored suit, wide smile, and he was in the process of stepping out on the town with his shiny new cane.

There were a total of seven of these elaborate poster advertisements, interspersed with original artwork. Each oil painting was affixed with the artist's name and the title of the piece on the frame. "The Sick Child," by Edward Munch, "Vase with Poppies," by Vincent Van Gogh, "Surrender of Santa Ana," by William Henry

135

Huddle, and "The Wrath of the Seas," by Ivan Alvazovsky.

"Sergeant Knowles and Mrs. Murphy?"

She was startled by the voice behind them. The slow drawl of the bass sound had a haunting quality.

When she turned around, the man she confronted was a short, bespectacled, and almost dwarfish character. He wore a white, plantation owner's suit with a black bowed tie and thick, pomaded gray hair. His hair style was swept back on the sides, with a distended pompadour that hung over his forehead like the veranda of his white mansion.

"Please. Come in the back. I have something I want to show y'all."

He turned on his heels and marched into the library. She looked over at Sarah and raised her eyebrows. They followed after him.

Upon an easel was a square sheet of paper. On the paper was printed an organizational structure. He picked a teacher's pointer up from the library table and walked over to the chart.

"Be seated."

He pointed to the top box in which the name "World's Veterans" was printed inside it.

She wondered why he was showing them this information without first having asked for the Veterans' Administration paperwork of the fictional Arthur Knowles.

"I, Goodrich Lightfoot the third, come from one of the four thousand families in this great country of ours fortunate enough to own most of the wealth. We lucky four-thousand don't own all of the capital, mind you, but we do possess a great majority of it. My relatives, the Lightfoots of Virginia, go all the way back to the United States Revolution. George Washington's wife, Martha, as a matter of fact, lived in our first White House plantation, located not far from here."

"Dr. Lightfoot. I have Sergeant Knowles' veteran's papers. Would you care to see them?"

She pulled the copies out of her handbag and thrust them toward him.

"No. Not yet. This is more important right now. Y'all can relax a bit. The war's over."

She liked how he said "ovah," as if the word were part of an official declaration of independence.

"Thank you, sir. You may continue."

She sat down next to Sarah, who had already limped over to a chair and sat down, keeping her knees wide apart in a masculine pose. She was also sucking on her teeth, she noticed.

"Two of our family's White Houses were burned to the ground. The first time was after my Granddaddy Goodrich, and his brother, Sherwood, sold it to Martha Washington's Custis family before the Revolutionary War. One of Martha's later relatives, Robert E. Lee, Commander of the Confederate Army, was occupying it for a time before our War Between the States. Invading General George McClellan, in 1862, was occupying it."

"Where did General Lee's family go?" She said.

"To Richmond. This White House, mind you, was where Martha, the initial First Lady, married George Washington. However, the Union decided to burn it to the ground because a traitor had lived inside it. Now. This is my point. Each time that other White House was burned down, the last time being in 1880, it was built again, but it was smaller each time."

She noticed he was crying. Were they crocodile tears?

"When I built my Fourth White House, in 1885, I was a retired veteran and former surgeon at the Fort Sumter Prison, known to you Union folks as Andersonville. When I began my businesses, and I built this fourth and final house, I made a vow to give all of my earnings to the world's veterans. All of them."

"Quite noble of you, Dr. Lightfoot," she said.

He moved the pointer to the next box down from the first. Inside this box it said *World Trade*.

Dr. Lightfoot smiled.

"My business ventures are worldwide. We are all connected by investments from not only the four thousand families in the United States of America, but thousands of other families from every developed civilization around the world."

"I suppose the telegraph and now the telephone have made that investment process much easier," she said.

"Indeed, young lady, they do."

He pointed to the box connected at the bottom. Inside it was printed *The World's Best Leaders Are Veteran Leaders.*

"When I give to veterans and the public, I expect something in return. For example, I have little slave cabins on the back acres of my land here. They serve as the emancipation homes for my addicted patients who live here for seven days. I give them daily injections of my Lightfoot Cure medication, and teach them the Mithras Way, and ninety-eight percent are cured of their addictions at the end of the week!"

Sarah spoke for the first time. Her gaze was dream-like and fascinated.

"I am addicted to dreams. Can you cure me, doctor?"

"Certainly, Mr. Knowles. All it takes is courage, my medicine, and a commitment to the Mithras Way of Life."

He stopped, placed the pointer down on the table and turned toward them.

"I put my chosen veterans to work for me in a variety of ways. You, for example, shall serve an important leadership role. Just as in the Bible. When we beat our swords into plowshares, we do it because we understand the hell on earth that war brings to civilizations, and we know we must stop it forever. Correct?"

She looked up at him. His eyes were tearing again, and his pinched face was flushed.

She glanced over at Sarah, who had stood up. Her eyes followed the actress as she limped over to the corner of the library.

Standing in the corner, about three feet tall, was an odd-looking statue.

She also rose to her feet and walked over to see what it was. The head was that of a lion roaring. The body was that of a nude man, and he had wings coming out of his shoulder blades and the back of his calves. Encircling him was a gigantic python, its head and forked tongue pointing directly at the lion's head.

***

The Army Medical Museum, 511 10th St. NW, Washington, D.C., 8:30 PM.

Around them both were dozens of boxes filled with folders. On each folder was the name of the veteran to whom the records inside belonged. She and Isaiah were staring down at two records. The one she was looking at said *Abercrombie, Hubert, Lieutenant, Union Army.*

The folder Isaiah was looking at said *Watterson, Henry, Colonel, Confederate States.*

"I want to make sense of this. It's too important for us to get confused."

She looked at Isaiah, and he nodded.

"Go ahead. You have the legal mind, Clara. Finish our little puzzle."

"When news that General Grant refused to exchange prisoners because the South wouldn't return Union Negro soldiers held prisoner, Abercrombie joins the Confederates when an offer is given to the Andersonville prisoners in 1864. That's when he fights during the Battle of Egypt Station in Mississippi, and Henry Watterson is one of the Southern officers in charge."

Isaiah takes a deep breath.

"Yes, he joined the Rebel side."

She nodded.

"After the battle, Abercrombie is found to have been one of the former prisoners who was placed on the Southern front lines during the battle and who refused to surrender."

Isaiah grunted, "Yup."

"Abercrombie believed he would stand a better chance fighting the Union. Instead, he was arrested, and several fellow prisoners poured gasoline on him inside the stockade and set him on fire. That's where he actually got his scars."

Isaiah was in his full scowl state of expression.

"That lying bastard! He told us he saved Negroes from their

burning shacks in Washington."

It was her turn to take a deep breath.

"Watterson is sympathetic, and they both decide to join a secret society of veterans after the war."

He nodded.

"Correct. Now if we can just find out the name of the group they joined."

***

Fourth White House, New Kent County, Virginia, 8:30 PM.

"Are you familiar with the Mithras religion?"

Dr. Lightfoot walked over to them. She looked down at him standing beside her. His eyes were blue, she noticed, and they were bloodshot. Perhaps he had been drinking or partaking of some other drug.

"No, I simply wanted to see what Mr. Knowles found curious. Are you a collector?"

Her heart was pounding, and she tried to maintain her equilibrium.

"Not quite, young ladies, but I am a believer."

When she saw the two men enter the library, holding pistols in their hands, she knew all of their plans had been for naught. The first gentleman was the tall figure of the journalist, Henry Watterson. The second was none other than Detective Hubert Abercrombie.

"Ladies, we want you to come with us back to Washington. We are having a celebration and a feast. Along with this Mithraism, we shall begin a new plan to obtain even a bigger amount of money for our veterans' fund."

He nodded to Watterson.

She watched, as the tall blonde former congressman and Kentucky editor marched over to the Divine Sarah, took hold of the front of her plaid shirt and tore it asunder, until she was standing in front of them, half as naked as the white statue in the corner.

140

"How much do you suppose Sarah Bernhardt, the world's most popular actress, will be worth, Mr. Watterson?"

She could hear Sarah begin to speak. The three men stood there, two of them with guns, and one, the older doctor, with his mouth agape.

"I have often been asked why I am so fond of playing male parts. As a matter of fact, it is not male parts, but male brains that I prefer."

She, in spite of herself, began to laugh.

Chapter 12: Equilibrium

Oak View/Red Top, Corner of Macomb and 35th Streets, Georgetown Heights, May 17, 1887.

Moses Fleetwood Walker had the dream after they released him from the insane asylum at St. Elizabeths Hospital. The next morning, he knew he must contact the First Lady, Frances Cleveland, to discuss it. She told him over the school's telephone that she also had a dream, and she asked him if it were about the day they had met on Meridian Hill. When he told her it was, she said he should come out to Red Top to meet with her. He agreed.

There were still armed guards at the Cleveland's private residence, and they searched him very carefully before allowing him to go up to the big, red-roofed house. The two Secret Service men who met him at the front door also searched his body, even more closely, for weaponry.

"Can't be too careful, my boy," the older one said, smiling at him.

He was used to this kind of treatment, even while playing baseball. Umpires in the South often patted him down, saying they were looking for tools he might use to doctor the baseball of his pitcher, but he knew it was simply harassment because of his color.

In the back of the house, Mrs. Cleveland greeted him with open arms. Truth be told, he never hugged a more beautiful white woman in his life. She pointed to a rocking chair near the window of the sewing room, and she sat down on the flowered divan facing him.

The springtime morning sunlight was pouring in on her face as she smiled at him. As he looked up at the wedding painting, hanging on the wall, of her and her husband, he felt a bit strange. He was much closer in age to her than the portly, middle-aged president.

"Mr. Walker, I believe I know the location where I was held captive. The memories came flooding back to me, in my dream, but I wanted to discuss the idea with you first. My insight is based on

142

the terms used by my captors when they believed I was sufficiently drugged to not be consciously aware."

He could see she was nervously picking at a lock of black hair on her forehead.

"Go on. I shall compare it with what I dreamt," he responded.

"It was actually an argument I overheard going on between two of my captors. In my mind, I was visualizing a bullfight I witnessed in Spain, and the Picadors were piercing the flesh of the poor bull, and I could hear its caterwaul as the voices of the two Picadors spoke to each other about the bull."

She leaned forward, and he could see the mounds of her white breasts, so he self-consciously focused upon her blue eyes, which were quite riveting as well.

"One was saying that the shot came to the back of the head, from fifteen feet behind. In my mind's picture, however, I saw the Picador demonstrating his thrust at the bull from behind his horned head. The image and the conversation did not match."

"I understand the feeling," he said.

"And then … when the other Picador spoke, my newly awakened mind knew where they were keeping me captive."

"Go ahead, Mrs. Cleveland. What did he say?"

He leaned forward to listen.

"He said that the doctor paid Mr. Booth to do the job right. He said Booth was not more than five feet from Lincoln's head as the president watched the play."

"Don't you think you might have been dreaming that because your husband was president? Lincoln's assassination might have been on your mind," he pointed out.

"No, it was real, and it was happening," she replied.

"Do you believe it was really happening exactly where you were?"

He was thinking about his own dream at that moment.

"Yes. I believe it's based on reality because I remember that I distinctly felt the muzzle of cold steel at the back of my head at that same moment. I think I was being used as a replacement to show where President Lincoln was shot in the head."

He decided to tell her about his dream.

"My dream envisioned you being marched toward me by armed soldiers. You were still blindfolded, and at first I thought they were going to execute you. But then, I saw Detective Abercrombie and the white journalist, Mr. Watterson. They told the men to leave."

"They could have been the men who arrested you at Meridian Hill," she replied.

"No. It was a dream because when I stepped forward and looked closely at you, the blindfold you wore, I could see, was actually constructed of hundreds of white spiders clinging together by their legs."

"How ghastly!"

"I awoke at that point. You must understand, Mrs. Cleveland. When I was questioned at the jail, it was all dark in the room except for a bright light shining into my eyes. They were telling me about spiders that had overtaken the Treasury Department's buildings."

"Were they trying to frighten you?"

"I believe so. It was then I began to have my hallucination about the white demons who were starting to begin slavery once more."

Her eyes became wide again.

"My goodness, Mr. Walker. You just made me remember something."

"Remember what?"

Did she know about the white demons also?

"Mrs. Caroline Taylor once told me the same thing. She said the white demons spin lies and have come to entrap us in their webs of sin. She told me she believed we should understand Isaiah 59:6: *Their webs will not serve as clothing; men will not cover themselves with what they make. Their works are works of iniquity, and deeds of violence are in their hands.*"

He stood up.

"What is the building in which you believe you were held prisoner?"

"The old Ford's Theater on 10th Street. That was where President Lincoln was shot. My captors were discussing his execution. It is now the Army Medical Museum."

She stood up.

"And the spiders dwell within," he said.

"Mr. Palmary! We must go to Washington at once," she shouted.

As they pulled away from Red Top in the carriage, with the two Secret Service agents, he realized there was a way to "fight fire with fire," as his father had always termed it.

"Mrs. Cleveland, if the white demons are swarming now, we need to be careful. They might kill the hostages if we storm the barricades."

She looked at him with those blue eyes again. He wondered if they harbored a secret displeasure at his forthright behavior. Instead of snapping back at him, she smiled.

"Yes, I can see how that might be true, Mr. Walker. What do you propose we do?"

She touched his hand.

"What is the date today?"

His mind returned to his occupational inspiration. Whenever he was on the road playing baseball, his every move was dictated by the date and time of the game being played.

"It's Tuesday. May 17."

"Please take me to Swampoodle Grounds. The Nationals are playing at home today. There is someone there I want to see before we go to the museum. He may be able to assist us in conducting a subterfuge."

"Now there's a good vocabulary word for my students at the Home for Friendless Colored Girls. Subterfuge. A secret plan."

She craned her lovely ivory neck out of the carriage window and shouted up at the colored driver.

"Jasper! Take us to the ball game at Swampoodle first!"

***

145

The Army Medical Museum, 511 10th St. NW, Washington, D.C., 4:00 PM.

Clara and Isaiah returned to the museum the following afternoon. After discussing their dilemma with Dr. McFarland, they had come to the conclusion that the kidnappers were located somewhere inside the old Ford Theater, now the Army Medical Museum and Pension Records Building. Somehow, this group was using an ancient cult religion and drugs to control women and, most likely, veterans, to accomplish illegal acts like murder and kidnapping.

Captain Lees suggested they attempt to find the hideout on their own, as he knew having fifty or more police officers rampaging inside the building would force the kidnappers to kill young David immediately. Sleuthing on their own, however, they could search with much more discretion.

She was worried about not hearing from Laura Gordon or Sarah Bernhardt. On the buggy ride over from the hotel to the museum, she told Isaiah her concerns.

"What if Laura and Sarah were found out? Do you think the kidnappers would kill them?"

She searched Isaiah's scowling face for a reaction. He scowled even more.

"No. Get that thought out of your mind. Use your reason. If they discovered the identity of Sarah Bernhardt, they would realize how valuable she could be to them. I would wager she is worth ten times the ransom money they obtained for the First Lady. Don't you agree?"

She exhaled.

"I suppose you're correct. But how do you plan to overpower these people? There must be at least two or three of them. Also, what about Jerimiah? If he is part of their group, then what role does he play?"

"If Dr. McFarland is correct, your former husband is jolly well motivated by sex, drugs, money, and this Mithras balderdash. Quite a potent combination. Don't you agree?"

She noticed that Isaiah's British accent still entered his speech at stressful moments.

"Aha. So, you *do* agree the tattoos were given to the women because they were performing as sex slaves?"

They pulled up to the front of the museum. The driver, an old colored man, opened the door for her. She stepped onto the ladder and held the man's hand to step down to the sidewalk. She looked back at Isaiah to hear his response.

"In my experience, the best criminals use the same motivators our society uses to influence us. Therefore, yes. Sex is the biggest influential motivator."

He stepped down after her and broke his scowl with a brief grin.

"I see you were also distracted by the mention of sex. So much so, you failed to answer my first question. How will we overpower these rogues once we discover where they are? Our main suspects are Detective Abercrombie and the journalist, Henry Watterson."

When they entered the museum's main entrance, Isaiah opened the door for her. As he did so, he pulled away his coat to flash his Bowie knife, the black handle with the cobra pattern rising out of its leather sheath. It was the hidden companion to the Colt .45 in the holster around his waist.

"I do not plan to use these, unless we must. As soon as we can discover the hidden room where they are, or even see Abercrombie or Watterson present at all, we shall notify the authorities at once."

"Agreed. We must use all five senses to ferret out these devils. In fact, we must not let Abercrombie or Watterson know that we are prowling for their hide away. To them, we are searching pension records for one of your veteran friends in San Francisco."

She grasped Isaiah's right arm, at the crook, and walked with him up to the clerk's desk, where a uniformed soldier was on duty.

The soldier informed them that he was going to lock and close the museum doors, for the time being, but he would let them out later.

147

***

The Army Medical Museum, 511 10th St. NW, Washington, D.C., 4:15 PM, Within the Mithraeum.

Laura tried to use her four senses when they were transported from the Fourth White House plantation in New Kent County to their present location. A gun was kept against their sides when they traveled by train to the Union Depot in Washington. When they were transferred to the carriage, Abercrombie and Watterson affixed blindfolds and handcuffs upon them, and they rode the final distance in silence.

She was escorted along what felt to be a cement or brick path, and she could distinctly hear the sounds of street traffic, smell the odor of horse manure, and feel the breeze off what she surmised was the Potomac. She assumed they were somewhere in the city, but she could not ascertain an exact location. They might be in most any of Washington's more metropolitan areas.

"Are you all right, Miss Bernhardt?" She spoke to her friend, whose steps she could hear beside her, accompanied from behind by what sounded like the boots of several men.

"Thus far, I feel like a blindfolded Horatio. I fear we shall see worse things than ghosts and skulls, however, Prince Hamlet."

"I am gladdened to hear your sense of humor has not been restrained. Clara always says I have too much of the mechanical mind of an attorney. If she could only see me now."

They were led down into what was a much damper, colder, and more enclosed passageway. She could smell the dusty odor of books or other documents. They might be inside a library or perhaps a book warehouse.

She tripped on something, but she felt a strong hand grip her by the scruff of her nurse's uniform to keep her standing. When it seemed they had finally arrived at their destination, she was standing still, waiting for the next revelation.

"Take their blindfolds off, gentlemen."

The voice with the Southern drawl was speaking.

When the thick black cloth was removed from her eyes, she could not, at first, see. Gradually, the blurry darkness revealed flickering gas lamps on the walls, and then she could see several religious images that made her conclude that Clara and Dr. McFarland had been correct. She and Sarah were now in the center of an underground Mithraeum cave of worship.

The entire cave took up at least 100 yards of underground space, but only the central area was lit. Around them, in the darkness, she could only guess what might lie in wait within the damp confines of the rest of the cave. She could hear what sounded like bells tinkling in the near distance.

They had been placed in the center of the cave, on a raised marble platform, like chess pieces on a board, in front of what appeared to be an altar. Clara, whose father was a Protestant minister, had always told his daughter that the early Catholics saw the altar as the place where the literal body and blood of Jesus Christ was transubstantiated and offered to the celebrants.

This altar, however, was adorned from behind the stone sacrificial table with the embossed, graven tableau of Mithras, performing his tauroctony. The center-piece was Mithras clothed in an Anatolian costume and wearing a Phrygian cap. He was kneeling on the exhausted bull, holding it by the nostrils with his left hand, and stabbing it with his right. As he did so, he looked over his shoulder towards the figure of Sol, the sun. A dog and a snake reached up towards the spouting blood. A scorpion seized the bull's genitals. A raven was flying around the bull. Three ears of wheat were growing out from the bull's wound.

Their four escorts, standing next to the altar, wore white gowns, with headdresses that came to a three-sided, pointed edge, similar to the top of the Washington Monument. She guessed it was Dr. Lightfoot's body under the sheet closest to the stone altar. The top of his pointed head came even with the platform's flat surface, whereas the three other ghost-like figures were taller, although one was only a few inches taller than Lightfoot. Each of these three men held a repeating rifle.

Dr. Lightfoot's right hand was resting upon the shoulder of

a much taller rendition of the statue they saw at the Fourth White House. The lion-headed, winged naked man, with the python encircling his body. She suspected they were now going to be given a grand lecture about why they were here.

"Around the world, inside caves such as this, many more celebrants are now offering up their sacrifices to Mithras. These celebrants are of the white, upper classes, and their servants are the ones we control. They, like the rest of ignorant mankind, exist above, in the turmoil and confusion caused by the quest for wealth and power. They do not know that it is we who control everything from below."

"Hail, Mithras!"

She heard the others shout.

"We build our temples below theirs. In fact, this structure will soon move to a much larger edifice housing all the records of our glorious warriors. These warriors continue fighting to keep the wheels of profit revolving, forever, as long as life sustains us. Only afterward, when they retire, do they become vulnerable to our methods. We offer them new fame, new money, and a new chance to serve us above, as we control them from below. If the government refuses to serve them, then we shall! Bring in the child and the dancing seductresses of the Mithraeum, the Goddesses of Dependencies!"

She could see them come from the darkness of the cave behind them. There was a line of four harem women, a drummer, and a trumpeter that came from the right. The line of two men and the one boy came from the left.

The boy, whom she surmised was David, was handcuffed, as they were, but he still wore his blindfold. She could not recognize the two men, also in white gowns and hoods, who accompanied him.

The four women began to dance, weaving a snake-like rhythm, each striking a bell-laden tambourine above her head with her hand. Their midnight veils and silk gowns undulated upon their nude bodies like waves, as they pranced and raised their legs high to the tune of the trumpet's blare and the tambourines' beat. She could see that each dancer had the same tattoo of the roaring lion-headed man etched into the small of her back.

"Give them all the Mithras Elixir!"

One of the dancers, accompanied by a hooded armed escort, walked over to a small table on wheels that had several syringes laid out on a white cloth. First, the dancer rolled the table over to the blindfolded David Milton. He was given an injection. Then, the dancer rolled over to Sarah Bernhardt, and the escort pointed his rifle at her as the dancer gave the actress the injection. Finally, the table rolled over to her, and the dancer picked up another syringe, held it aloft, grabbed her arm, and injected the long needle into her bicep.

She could see that the red trumpet being played was in the shape of the Angel's Trumpet flower. The drum had Sandalwood incense pouring out of it. As it was struck, smoke poured forth, in wavy swaths of gray mist. As she watched, she began to feel a new passion rise in her chest and travel to her limbs.

"Strip the lawyer for the sacrifice!"

Dr. Lightfoot shouted and pointed toward her. She wondered if she were going to be the sacrifice or just an observer.

Two of the riflemen marched over, came to a halt, and pointed their guns at her head. She felt her knees weaken, and her heartbeat and breathing changed from rhythmic passion to explosive terror.

"Disrobe!" They shouted at her.

Slowly, she took off each layer of her blue nurse's costume, until the last piece, her pantaloons, were lying on top of the pile on the marble tiles. She stood there, shivering, hands at her side, half-expecting some judge to tell her she was out of order.

The drug must have begun to work, as halos began to form above each of the heads of the people, and she felt a pleasant calm enter her body. She thought that life itself must be an intricate game of hide-and-seek between angelic beings. She reached above her own head, but she could feel nothing.

Dr. Lightfoot ordered, "I want that Jewess to sing and dance to the song of Mithras and the sacrifice!"

The other rifleman marched over to Sarah, pointed his rifle

at her head, and she disrobed. She noted that even though the Divine Sarah was the world's greatest actress, now that she stood naked, she was shivering, and her dark eyes were wide with embarrassed fear. She covered her breasts with her right arm, and she covered her vagina with her left hand, in abject shame.

Dr. Lightfoot shouted, and his voice echoed inside the sonorous confines.

"Take the boy's blindfold off. Sergeant Foltz, I want your son to see how committed we are to our goal. Remove your hood as well!"

***

The Army Medical Museum, 511 10th St. NW, Washington, D.C., 4:15 PM, Above the Mithraeum.

Clara envisioned the theater all around her. Despite the walls containing stacks and boxes filled with government pension files; despite the grubby dispassion of military ennui and record-keeping; she could sense the life of many dramas, which had been played out within this tomb of a disastrous war's climax.

Perhaps Lincoln's spirit was fighting with Booth's spirit for territory beyond humanity's veil of tears. She believed now that the violence and struggle never ended, despite the hopes and dreams of mothers, of their children, and of their peace-loving fathers.

She watched one such peace-lover, her Isaiah, turn the corner at a row up ahead. She heard the sound, and her mind pictured a most ridiculous image. She once more saw the scene Laura had described inside the Medical Museum, when Sarah, playing Prince Hamlet, had hopped upon Isaiah's back. There was the sound of a man's voice bursting forth with an "oof" and then of a large body striking against the wood shelves all around them.

When she rounded the same corner, however, a rifle was pointed at her head, and she saw Isaiah lying on the floor, unconscious, a stream of blood gushing from a wound at his right temple. The violent ghosts of Ford's Theater had finally come to life. And the drama was real.

As she was being escorted down the ladder, into the bowels of the building, she kept looking backward to find Isaiah, who was being dragged by a husky soldier, still unconscious and disarmed. Were these soldiers working at the pension office as employees of the government, or were they fellow conspirators of the kidnappers?

***

The Army Medical Museum, 511 10th St. NW, Washington, D.C., 4:25 PM, Within the Mithraeum.

When they took the blindfold from his face, David Milton wanted to see only one person. His father. For days, he heard his voice all around him; felt his touch when he was bathed and fed; smelled his cologne as his father read to him.

But the first persons he saw were the naked bodies of two women he knew very well. His mother's best friend and legal partner, Laura Gordon, and his personal idol and exemplar, the Divine Sarah Bernhardt. They both were shaking from the cold, and Miss Bernhardt was trying to cover herself with her hands and arms.

The other people and details meant little to him, other than the interesting costumes the dancers were wearing and the strange, hooded white uniforms of the men holding the rifles.

His father, who was also holding a rifle, had been instructed to take his hood off, so he was the only one of the ghostly characters he could identify. The shortest of these men, who had no gun, was giving the orders, and this man stood beside a flat marble altar with a square design of a man killing a bull, in the midst of other animals, serving as a background.

"Bring the Jew whore a dress. What will you sing for us as you dance? As we used to tell our slaves in Virginia, you can sing for your supper."

A pleasing relaxation began to fill his mind. His eyelids felt heavy, and a soothing warmth entered his limbs. He wondered if this were all a drama in which his idol was the star. Perhaps they would all go home afterward, the way they were supposed to do before he was kidnapped at the National Theater. In that play, she had been a

153

princess. In this drama, she was a dancing slave. What was his part going to be?

There was a grinding noise above, and soon he could see stairs being lowered to the ground of their basement. What followed was a procession of three Army soldiers in uniform. One was escorting a woman and the two others were dragging a man. When they finally came into the light of the lamps in the center of the stage, he could see who they were. The woman was his mother, and the man was Captain Lees. They must be part of the show.

The soldier guarding his mother came over to the short ghost and began to whisper where his ear must be located under the hood. The short man nodded, and the guard left, floating up the steps from where he had come.

The short man stepped out into the center of the platform. When he spoke, it was as if his voice came from everywhere in the room.

"Ladies and gentlemen! We are going to have an addition to our celebration. One of my business partners, who works in Chinatown, has sent over four ceremonial lions to dance for us. When they have finished, I shall begin the offering to Mithras."

He could feel the vibration from the metal stairs, and the red and gold animals that came down filled his consciousness with the sound of Chinese chanting. As soon as the four lions stepped upon their center platform, they began to dance. Each lion had a wide head with bulging eyes. Their bodies shivered in the lights, and their heads shook like a male lion roaring. The colors were gold and red, and he could see there were four human legs beneath each lion's costume.

Dancing next to them were the Divine Sarah and the four harem women. One of the lions came over to Sarah and she nodded her head at something she heard from it. It must have been a magical incantation, because the Divine Sarah began to sing a song:

> *When these pillars get pulled down,*
> *It will be you who wears a crown,*
> *And I'll owe everything to you.*

He recognized the song as an English translation of an aria from Camille Saint-Saens' opera, *Samson and Delilah*. He watched, as she spun her body around and around and moved in slow, weaving steps over to where the short ghost was standing.

How much pain has cracked your soul?
How much love would make you whole?
You're my guiding lightning strike.

She pursed her red lips and pressed them against his white hood. He saw that her kiss left a mark.

I can't find the words to say,
But they're overdue,
I've traveled half the world to say,
I belong to you.

"Bring him to me. We must begin the offering."

Two of the tall ghosts with rifles walked over to him. Each took one of his arms, and they marched him over to the altar. They lifted him up and placed him on the platform above the altar. Four silver bracelets came out of the stone altar and encircled his wrists and his ankles. He stared up into the darkness, and he could see hundreds of spider webs suspended between the wood beams.

The voice again filled the cavern.

"Our economy is a connection of entrepreneurial webs. Each web is controlled by a Mithras soldier, who has been spiritually transformed after the wars into an independent, holy spider. Each spider must regain mastery over the subhuman species of tribal niggers and those free-spirited gadflies who gave them freedom. Each spider is filled with the Mithras Elixir, and each web catches the unwary citizen who still believes in the emancipation of those who must remain slaves to our divine right of control. One by one, we shall capture them, inject them, and trap them."

He watched, in fascinated wonder, as the beams above him

began to descend. As they came closer, he could see hundreds of writhing spiders, clinging and pulsing together, waiting to be released upon contact with his face, torso, and legs.

"Hail Mithras! Hail Ye Goddesses of Dependencies!"

He turned his head, but he felt no fear, he simply wanted to protect his eyes and mouth, and then he saw a strange sight. The heads of the four dancing lions flew up into the air, as if they had been released as the spiders above him were to be. In each of the eight Negro women's hands was a rifle.

The streaking flashes of light erupted from the guns, and he looked for his father. In a scene out of a nightmare, he saw that his father was supine on the marble platform. He had been struck by a bullet from one of the guns, and he was lying on the altar, blood pouring from his body. That's when he felt the silver clasps around his wrists and ankles release him.

The guns were still blazing away at each other as the short ghost dragged him off the altar, down to the ground, and whisked him away, into the darkness beyond the central stage.

"Where's David?"

He could hear his mother's voice behind him, as he was being dragged into the ever-widening darkness.

"Mother! I'm here!"

He shouted, but they had come to a ladder, and he was being pulled up each wrung, step by step, into the brightness above them. When he finally reached the top, the ghost folded up the ladder, and the trap door to the depths below was shut.

His mind became a dreamscape of fantastic images. As the ghost pulled his arm, he could see hundreds of demonic body parts, soaked in liquid vats. There were gleaming white skulls and skeletons dancing on wires. Some of them rose out of the wooden tables, some peered at him from behind glass prisms, their distorted eye sockets black and hollow, and their gaping mouths grinned at him.

There were instruments of torture, which spread arms and legs apart, and twisted into the folds of the human brain, and knives of every size and shape that were plunged into the chests of full-sized, naked bodies. Silver razorblades blinded his eyes with their sharp, gleaming edges.

"Where do you think you're going?"

He saw one of the two phantoms standing before them. In what seemed like a moment of clarity, he could see that the man was not a ghost. He was a slender Negro, and he was a head taller than the very pretty woman standing at his side. He was holding a rifle. Two other men in dark suits, standing in the shadows, were pointing pistols at his ghostly escort.

His captor was unarmed, so he surrendered. He watched, as the handsome Negro came up to the ghost and yanked off his hood.

"You are under arrest for the kidnapping of Frances Cleveland, David Foltz, Laura Gordon, Sarah Bernhardt, Clara Foltz and Captain Isaiah Lees."

The short man in white laughed. His voice was no longer filling up the room with its volume.

"You have no proof. I have an explanation for all of this. I was saving this child from an illegal exercise of religious skullduggery. The only way I could do this was to infiltrate its inner sanctum."

The woman spoke, "Secretary Garland! You're the one behind all of this?"

Chapter 13: Going Home

Willard Hotel, Main Dining Room, 1401 Pennsylvania Ave. NW, Washington, D. C., May 18, 1887, 2:00 PM.

Clara purchased the train tickets for everyone, and she was seated at their rectangular table, gazing out the window at the brothels across the street. Perhaps it would be best for her to explain the connections between all the disparate parts of this unique case by first discussing how the lion dancers, under the employment of one Dante Cross of New Jersey, came into the picture. When she learned about this and the fact that Mrs. Caroline Taylor told Frances Cleveland about the spiders in the bible, she was eager to inform the others.

The only one of her team who did not experience some kind of traumatic event at the conclusion of their investigation was Dr. McFarland. Although, he did have his problems arguing with the attorney general about the sanity of Moses Fleetwood Walker. In addition, it was Dr. McFarland who broke the case open with his information about the Mithras religion.

"Ladies and Gentlemen. Please. I know you have a lot of questions, and we shall have the opportunity to discuss much of what I will cover during our long journey back to San Francisco."

Five of her San Francisco family were there, including Jerimiah Foltz, who survived his ordeal in the museum and had a bullet removed from his right shoulder. He was bandaged now and smiling up at her as she stood at the podium off to the side. David Milton was seated beside him. She needed her notes to be able to cover all the elements of this intricate mystery. Jerimiah and David were the only ones not talking.

"Please! Let me begin."

Silence.

"I want to first thank our guest, the First Lady, Frances Cleveland."

Everybody applauded, and the beautiful young woman

beamed her approval at them. She again wore one of her scandalously low and bare-front dresses. Clara's daughter, Trella Evelyn, said in a letter that she was going to wear this style "in honor of this trail-blazing and modern female." Trella and Frances were, after all, the same age.

"With Mrs. Cleveland's information about her friend, and victim, Mrs. Caroline Taylor, I was able to conclude that when Taylor spoke with my former client, Eloise Strong, at the D. C. Jail, their conversation was in biblical code. They were agreeing to report what they knew about the Mithras group and their use of drugs to keep them enslaved. As we now know, all three victims had the same tattoo on the small of their backs. They all must have been controlled with drugs by this secret group."

Laura raised her hand, and Clara nodded at her friend. "So, how did the kidnappers find out Strong, Taylor and perhaps Matron Scully were going to inform the authorities?"

"We now know that Detective Abercrombie and Mr. Watterson were part of the Mithras group. When Abercrombie found the transcriptions of the seven who visited Miss Strong, he began to suspect what the coded message meant between Mrs. Taylor and Miss Strong. He had already told me that Scully and Strong had a strange affinity."

"All of them had to be disposed of before they could report what they knew to the White House."

Isaiah was voicing his usual superb complement to her detective logic, and she smiled down at him. "You are quite correct, Captain," she said.

"Of course, we would have never been able to solve this case at all without the bravery and insightful genius of the first man to break the color barrier in professional baseball, Mr. Moses Fleetwood Walker."

Again, the company applauded, and Mr. Walker hung his head. He had to play a game in New Jersey the following day, as he told her, but he would not have missed this luncheon for the world.

"I would like to explain how we were able to narrow our search for the kidnappers. As most of you are aware, we followed the clues where they led us. Detective Abercrombie and his cohort, Henry Watterson, attempted to lead us down one path, but, thanks to the research of Laura Gordon and Dr. McFarland, we began to fit together a more complex puzzle."

"I wanted to ask Mr. Walker something," said Isaiah, who had his head bandaged from the blow he took from an Army rifle butt.

"Are you certain you can make a decipherable sentence, Captain?" Dr. McFarland chuckled.

"Yes. I am quite conscious now. Thank you, doctor. Moses, how did you and Mrs. Cleveland come upon the same location that our group discovered? You had no knowledge about Dr. Lightfoot and the veterans. And you certainly weren't aware of the Mithras religion."

Moses shook his head. "I really don't know how to explain it except for the fact that the First Lady and I had similar dreams, or supernatural intuition, concerning the kidnappers and their location."

Mrs. Cleveland raised her hand, and Clara nodded at her.

"I was able to extract information about the assassination of President Lincoln from a conversation I overheard, in a drug-induced state, during my time as a captive. I knew Ford's Theater was where Lincoln was shot. In addition, like the biblical Joseph, Mr. Walker was able to intuit his own dream information about there being military men involved in my captivity. However, it was his subterfuge involving Mr. Dante Cross that proved to be the *pièce de résistance*. If I am using that term correctly."

Sarah Bernhardt, who was wearing a man's double-breasted blue suit, smiled at her.

"*Bon, c'est correct, madame.*"

"Mr. Walker," the First Lady turned to Moses. "Perhaps you can continue?"

He smiled and nodded at Mrs. Cleveland. She could tell they had a mysterious affinity.

"I knew Cross was gambling at the ball game out at Swampoodle Grounds, so we stopped there before heading to the museum. When I told him that Abercrombie and Watterson were blaming him for the kidnapping, he became quite angry. That's when he offered the services of the eight trained women from Chinatown, near Murder Row. They were quite proficient with repeating rifles as well as doing the Lion Dance. Let us say it was our gift to the celebration, and since Cross had worked with Dr. Lightfoot in the past, he knew where they held the Mithras meetings, and the group allowed the dancers to participate."

"Brilliant! Now I must ask Clara the multi-million-dollar question. Why weren't Attorney General Garland and Dr. Lightfoot arrested and put on trial?"

Isaiah always had the difficult questions, but she was ready with her answer.

"In deference to our First Lady, I must admit that when I saw President Cleveland shake hands with both Dr. Lightfoot and Augustus Garland, after they were detained, I remembered the 'mitra,' or the so called 'gentlemen's agreement' that Dr. McFarland pointed out as the true source of groups like the Roman Mithras cult."

"You can't believe my husband is involved in my own kidnapping, Mrs. Foltz." Frances Cleveland's face was flushed.

"No, not quite. But I do believe that our entire country today worships at the altar of greed, and those who control the most capital are our idols. In fact, the murder of Judge Marshal Owens was initiated by a young woman who was so drug-addled and dream-laden that she believed she could improve her lot in life by paying such homage to a man she thought could break those unseen barriers to success and achievement. I told the president about the speech Garland gave at the underground Mithraeum built by his followers, and how he brought those spiders down upon my son's face."

"Mother, don't forget about how he forced Mrs. Gordon and the Divine Sarah to disrobe and dance!" David Milton shouted.

"Yes. However, as President Cleveland assured me, all of it was permitted by using the legal cloak of our First Amendment and its freedoms. He and his Justice Department believed that Garland was attempting to rescue you, David. As for Lightfoot, he is beyond reproach, as nothing can connect him to the plot of the kidnappers other than Sarah and Laura. Since they were, technically, invited to celebrate a secret springtime religious festival of Mithras, they were not being kidnapped, they were believed to be official guests at a religious ceremony."

She could see that Laura was furious, so she nodded at her before she exploded.

"How can they do that? We made every connection. The poisons. The three dead victims. The drugs that were used to turn women into sex slaves and veterans into automatons. What did they say to that information?"

She shook her head slowly at her partner.

"I am afraid they saw all of that as circumstantial evidence. The veteran the First Lady saw at the jail and the one I saw at the Home for Friendless Colored Girls were never found. The arrested employees at the Army medical museum were, along with Detective Abercrombie and Mr. Watterson, on Lightfoot's payroll. And there was one other man."

"Who was that?" Laura was still frowning.

"Nathan Bedford Forrest."

It was Isaiah's turn to erupt.

"The rebel Lieutenant General whose cavalry attacked Fort Pillow in April of '64?"

She nodded at Isaiah.

"When that demon on horseback saw that the fort was manned by the colored infantry, most of those boys he and his men captured were slaughtered. I remember that the coloreds in other regiments soon began yelling 'Remember Fort Pillow' whenever they went out to battle."

"I'm sorry, Isaiah. He is now considered a civilian under the law," she replied. "Sadly, just as groups like the Ku Klux Klan are seen as patriotic avengers, so too is this Mithras group being seen by the media as a group that protects the rights of white men."

"I understand now," Isaiah said. "The only ones who will be prosecuted are the automaton vets. Abercrombie, Watterson, Forrest, and the workers at the museum. I know how all that works.

They'll all get suspended sentences, as long as they return the money they got from the gems."

Dr. McFarland cleared his throat.

"I was meaning to ask. This veterans' ruse they planned so deviously. I don't expect the retired vets, like Jerimiah, got any of that money, correct? They must work for a pittance. And, of course, there are those addictive drugs. The women and the vets were being controlled by addiction. What did they say to that?"

"I never saw any of that money," Jerimiah spoke for the first time. "Dr. McFarland is helping me overcome my addiction, and this is the only truth I have been given from this horrible experience."

She noticed he had the same vehement tone that had always frightened her when she was a young wife. However, today she saw that this tone was confident, and not arrogant, so she had agreed to allow David to visit him in San Jose, in the future, as long he was well supervised.

"The three women died from overdoses of the same drug, the Angel's Trumpet potion. We cannot prove it came from Dr. Lightfoot. The veterans, one of whom was outside the jail and another at the Home for Friendless Colored Girls, were supplying the poisons, but neither could be found."

Clara was especially angry that these fine women had died in vain.

Laura again raised her hand.

She nodded at her.

"If I had the time, I would also make a thorough investigation of those pension records. There were so many vetoes made by President Cleveland of independent congressional pension bills. I would wager this same group doctored some of those records to attempt to defraud the government. They are certainly doing it in the private sector. They want the Negroes and women to remain subservient. That is for certain."

She decided to let them hear the rest of her rancor. She was thinking of Jerimiah and Isaiah.

"I certainly believe we can add our veterans to the classes of

163

vulnerable citizens. It must be our duty to protect them and give them enough money and support to allow them to live when they are totally disabled and have served us in times of conflict. The same for our other groups. Women, Negroes, and immigrants. We are all at risk during these so-called peaceful times of white male greed and secret corruption."

She realized she was, once again, getting up on her soapbox. However, when the entire group began to applaud, she felt they all might have some hope for the future.

"What do you plan to do when you return to California?" Sarah Bernhardt said.

"I am going to get to work on my new plan for establishing a California Public Defender's Office," she explained.

"I would like to stay in correspondence with my new ingénue and understudy." Sarah smiled at David Milton.

"Oh, Miss Bernhardt! I would have danced with you in *Samson and Delilah*, but the spiders were coming toward me. That pipsqueak ghost had me trapped. Damn him!"

Sarah stood up and began to waltz over to where David Milton sat beside his father. She took his hands. He stood up, and he was wearing his mother's ruffled orange taffeta spring dress, with matching straw hat, medium bustle, and parasol. His shoes were orange with black heels.

"*Monsieur* Foltz, would you dance with me now?"

Everybody applauded, and Clara looked over at the hotel's waiter. He nodded his head and rushed into the kitchen.

After five minutes, three musicians, on a break from their playing in the ballroom, came into the dining room. One was a singer, one played the clarinet, and one played a violin.

"Miss Bernhardt? What shall we play?" The singer said.

"*Mon cœur s'ouvre à ta voix?* My heart opens itself to your voice?"

"*Oui, madamoiselle*," the singer said, and he began to hum, and the two musicians began to play.

Sarah, in her man's tailored suit, began to sing:
"*Dalila! Dalila! Je t'aime!* Dalilah, I love you!"

David sang the single refrain, and they circled each other out on the floor:

"*Samson! Samson! Je t'aime!* Samson, I love you!"

David sang, weaving around her, his red lips grazing her cheek each time she turned:

When these pillars get pulled down,
It will be you who wears a crown,
And I'll owe everything to you.

She reached for him, and he spun into her arms, singing:

How much pain has cracked your soul?
How much love would make you whole?
You're my guiding lightning strike.

She crooned to him, her face next to his:

"*Dalila! Dalila! Je t'aime!*"

He replied, his head back, in a swoon:

I can't find the words to say,
But they're overdue,
I've traveled half the world to say,
I belong to you.

She pressed her lips to his, and when she pulled away, he felt them with his fingers, knowing they were marked forever.

The next mystery in the Portia of the Pacific series is now being written. Here's the plot:

Penelope Farmer, an unwed sixteen-year-old daughter of a San Francisco merchant who, ironically, makes his fortune selling dangerous abortion drugs to lower class women, is impregnated. The girl is half-Navajo, and her mother, Haseya, has been dead for three years.

As a result, she seeks the help of a female midwife and abortionist. The abortion at 15 weeks goes wrong, and the girl is on her death bed. The police raid the clinic, and learn that the girl named Aloysius Farmer as the father of her child before she died. Since "death bed statements" are admissible evidence, when the girl dies, the midwife, Mrs. Honora Fulbright, is arrested, and the father is open to a civil lawsuit.

That's when Clara Foltz is hired by the father to defend him in civil court. Clara's adversary during the civil trial will be the San Francisco Protestant Orphan Asylum on behalf of all the public and private child welfare groups and homes throughout California. Aloysius Farmer is never accused of criminal rape or molestation. On the other side of town, Clara's partner, Laura Gordon, will be defending the midwife, Mrs. Honora Fulbright, who has been accused of manslaughter in the death of Penelope Farmer.

Here are the first three chapters from the upcoming Portia of the Pacific Legal Thriller Mystery, *Dark Justice*:

Dark Justice

Chapter 1: Journal Found in the Park

San Francisco California, Golden Gate Park, June 20, 1887.

M y name is Penelope Farmer. I am on my way to the clinic in Chinatown when I see the head of a crow. At first, I think it might be a voodoo doll, or charred food. It is lying on the path in front of one of the long benches in Golden Gate Park. I bend over to see it better. I can see the pitch-black head feathers, shiny with oil; the single eye, a milky film on its black pupil; the smoky-gray beak, opened slightly, as if the head has been lopped off mid-caw; no blood, no gore; just a warning message from one of my mother's Navajo dreams.

My mother, Haseya, which means "she rises," in the Navajo tongue, has been dead for three years. I was eleven at the funeral. I remember my mother teaching me about the power of dreams and tribal destiny. But my father says I need to learn to be a True Woman, without the superstitions and ghastly visions of my Native heritage. He appoints a private tutor, Mrs. Althea Crutchfield, who teaches me the basic skills of reading and math required for the True Woman of wealth. "Due to her emotional and physical frailty, a True Woman," according to Mrs. Crutchfield, "needs to be protected by a male family member. She is not supposed to think on her own, as that is the role of her protector and the other men of the Great Society."

Three years before my mother dies, when I am eight, my father is full of attentive love. He takes mother and I to all the best stores in San Francisco. He praises my progress in my lessons and buys me all the books I ask him to get me. He even takes us on a trip to Arizona territory, where father and mother first met on the reservation, and where my mother sold blankets and hand-crafted jewelry in the tribal store. That is when my mother first began to cough up blood, and I met her tribal medicine man. His name was Hástin Yázhe. He was tall, and he wore strange clothing. There was a young woman, also wearing native dress, who followed him all around, as if she were his shadow. He told me her name was Ajei and that she was a mute.

Shortly after the doctor in San Francisco says my mother has contracted consumption, our medicine man appears at our door. He says he has medicine to help us both. He tells Mrs. Crutchfield to give it to us both from now on, three times a day, after our meals. Mrs. Crutchfield was a nurse at one of the orphanage schools in which she taught, so she knows how to give us the three injections each day. My mother and I feel much better.

My mother even has a dream that first night we started our Navajo medicine. She sleeps beneath the Dream Catcher to prevent bad dreams. She says her husband, my father, Aloysius, is going to change. The week after this dream, she and I are working in the garden, and we see a coyote wandering on California Street next to our Nob Hill home. My mother screams and runs back into the house. But I stay, and I watch, entranced, as the ghostly gray cur begins to walk on his hind legs and then takes off, at great speed, running down the hill like a human. That same night my father begins to beat my mother after she fails to pay him proper respect. She screams and curses at him in Navajo, something she has never done before. I know she is dying, and she takes out all her anger and fear on him.

But one year later, on the night of a full moon, as I pull mother's body up on the pillow, I can feel her ribs under the night dress, and her breathing is a constant wheezing. Just as the moon radiates through the bedroom window upon her thin face, I see the long snout and white fangs of the coyote. My mother has transformed her voice into yips and yaps. That's when she first tells me about *yee naaldooshii*, the skinwalker we saw the week before in the front yard. We were both too afraid to speak of it until now. She tells me this creature is the tribal witch who can take the form of an animal and haunt a person who is inflicting harm upon someone in our tribe. As a result, Navajo Holy People wear only two animal skins, the sheepskin and the buckskin, and then only for ceremonial purposes. When I ask her into which animals the skinwalker can change, my mother says that it is usually a coyote, owl, fox, wolf or crow--although a skinwalker witch does have the ability to turn into any animal she chooses.

On the second night after the full moon, just before my mother dies of consumption, she asks me, her eleven-year-old daughter, to come close to the bed. When my mother moves her hand and brings it to her lips, I know she wants to whisper something, so I lean forward and I can feel her thin fingers form a circle around her lips against my ear. "I am *yee naaldooshii*," she says, yipping and spraying saliva. "And so are you," she whispers. The final vowels become a howling echo, and then my mother dies.

Three years later, when I am fourteen, my father begins to visit me at night. Outside, I can hear the coyote howl, and I begin to create my own myth, my personal Navajo legend. I am transformed into my mother, taking her place, and what father starts to do to me is because I am now possessed by the spirit of Haseya. During the day, as I do the chores, go shopping, instruct the mansion staff, everything, I do it just as mother did. And, in the bedroom at night, I can feel his probing hands, his great weight, his sweaty skin, and his kisses. I can hear his whispers of affection, his grunting, and can watch, with fascination, at the rising tumor below his waist. I am Haseya. One night, I bleed on the sheets for the first time. When he leaves, I stand at the bay window in my mother's night dress and howl at the coyote standing alone outside in the foggy San Francisco night. Perhaps I am not the *yee naaldooshii*, the skinwalker. I am protecting my father from the tribal curse.

Two years pass, and when I stop having my monthlies, at age sixteen, I am afraid to tell my tutor, Mrs. Crutchfield. She might take me off my Navajo medicine. Thereafter, the City Library becomes my only escape. Kind Mrs. McMillan, the Head Librarian, shows me all the books I need to learn about my body and how it functions. After I learn I am pregnant, I know I need to act, before it is too late. I start to read the newspapers. Among all my father's ads for female patent medicines, are other ads; they tell women about places to go where their "menses problems" can be addressed in person. Magic words like "vagina," "uterus," "umbilical cord," "placenta," and "still birth" fill my dreams, complete with the drawings from the books.

At first, I admit, I want to poison or hang myself. Killing myself seems to be the only solution. I am too ashamed to approach anyone about what is happening with my father. I read the articles about other girls and women in my same predicament; they break the laws, use abortifacients such as father sells, and then they become prostitutes. Often, they die at the hands of women like Madame Restell, in New York City, who is called the "Abortionist Vampire." The female abortionist's image in the *Police Gazette* is especially dreadful. Below Restell's haunting figure is a flying vampire, a baby held in its clenched jaws. In the article, the author quotes from Lord Byron's poem, *The Giaour*:

> "Thy victims ere they yet expire
> Shall know thy demon for their sire,
> As cursing thee, thou cursing them,
> Thy flowers are withered on the stem."

I am terrified of meeting such a person. Is she another kind of *yee naaldooshii?* Yet, after week fifteen, I become more horrified of my future than I am of my present.

I read other magazines, such as the *Woodhull and Claflin Weekly*, and *Revolution*, the Women's Suffrage magazine. The articles explain domestic incest, voluntary motherhood, rape, and the prosecution of women who have no legal rights. Men and parents can place their pregnant daughters into insane asylums, or imprison them in private hospitals, or force them to give birth and then steal the child from the mother, selling it on the open market through agencies. Church organizations can use these bastard children, as working slaves, inside orphanages.

These magazines understand my problem, so I call and make the appointment with Mrs. Honora Fulbright, a midwife. Fulbright advertises in one of the women's magazines, and she is the woman who is performing the procedure today. Mrs. Fulbright charges what I can afford, so I steal the money from my father.

Today, I am mentally distraught, and my Navajo medicine is making me see things. Finding this crow's head is especially macabre. As I am also an amateur ornithologist, I know about crows and their "murders." I know how crows track each other; like women, they form covens in which they share their experiences in a complex process of interpersonal communications. If one is injured on the ground, the entire murder will fly over its body, circling and cawing maniacally, until there are enough of them, and then they will land near their wounded comrade. They will watch after, protect, and feed the incapacitated one, sometimes for weeks, and their animosity toward approaching enemies is cunning and vengeful.

I realize that this crow's head is a spirit sign, from my dead mother, for me to meditate upon. A human enemy has done this, and crows remember their enemies. I also know the crow can be a *yee naaldooshii,* a skinwalker.

I sit down on the park bench, my ruffled blue dress blowing haphazardly in the ocean's winds. As I stoop over to view the crow's head, my small straw hat, with the thin elastic chin band, snaps off, and rises from my black hair, upward, floating toward the cumulus puffs high in the cobalt sky.

I stare down at the crow's head, and I close my eyes; in my vision, my body replaces the crow on the ground the same way I replaced my mother. Except, in my vision, I have no head, only a torso, arms and legs. From my dreamer omniscience, I look up. Flying around in concentric circles, instead of crows, are other women, and my body is in the center. Each woman is a personification of the different stages in a pregnancy. The ones, like me, at fifteen weeks, have small bumps protruding at their midsections. Others, if they are pregnant for the first time, begin to show that bump later, as their stomach muscles have yet to become stretched from previous births. Still other women are larger, each one soaring above, like a gigantic child's balloon, her stomach displaying the harbinger of future life, budding inside her womb, like the Truth itself.

The flying women disappear, and my father, Aloysius,

appears next. He is outside, in the garden, on Nob Hill. He never stands in the garden. There is a murder of crows flying just above his head. He reaches up, snatches one of the crows out of the air, and pulls it down to him. He yanks a knife from the sheath at his belt and holds the blade next to the squirming crow's neck. He stands, great and tall in his black top hat, tuxedo, and gleaming spats; he slices the head off the struggling crow; the head falls to earth, splattering speckles of blood on his white ankle covers; he curses and carries the crow's blood-spewing body inside the house. He walks resolutely over to the iron cauldron inside the pantry and drops it into the roiling water. This is where he makes his Dr. Goody's Female Menstrual Potions.

***

"Something's gone terribly wrong!" the girl screams.

Mrs. Fulbright stands at the end of the barber's chair in the kitchen, the metal probe in her gloved hands, her two children screaming next-door in the parlor.

The heroin tablets are working. The girl stares, in a mesmerized fog, down at the bloody sheet, which covers the lower half of her body. Her legs are spread wide apart, held in stirrups, and the blood is quickly soaking the sheet and the mattress beneath it.

The Chinese midwife doesn't know what to do. Her supervisor, Dr. Liu Wei, comes into the room from next-door. He frowns and turns toward her. The look on his face is both concerned and angry.

"What are you doing? Who is this child?" Dr. Liu Wei says.

They both watch the girl as she spreads her arms out, like a bird of prey, and screams, "My father, Aloysius Xavier Farmer, did this to me! He has impregnated his only daughter. I am not my mother. It is I, Penelope Farmer, and my death must be avenged!"

Chapter 2: Honor Lost

The Toy Mansion, Fifteen Nob Hill, San Francisco, June 23, 1887.

Trella Evelyn was home from college. She was reading in the library when the chimes told her somebody was at the front door of their new home. Mrs. Mary Hopkins, who had allowed them to stay with her at One Nob Hill for three years, had now become too demented to maintain her household. Her deceased husband's attorneys had taken over the mansion and forced all non-family members to find other accommodations.

Ah Toy, with a loan from her Uncle Pete, was able to purchase the new home at a reasonable price. They decided to save as much as they could, however, so while Trella and her four siblings were home for the summer, they would take turns doing the duties which would have normally fallen to the mansion's staff. Their grandparents, Elias and Talitha Shortridge, had moved back to San Jose.

Trella knew that most of the family was now part of their mother's detective and legal business, and Clara's new office was on the second floor. She and her siblings did not find the added encumbrance of acting as butlers, cooks, chauffeurs, and dish washers too demanding. In point of fact, they all wanted the chance to be part of any new case that might arise, as their mother's previous four cases were quite challenging.

As Trella walked out of the library, into the parlor, toward the front door, she adjusted the new green silk belt around her thin waist and tucked a lock of reddish-brown hair into her matching hair band. She was now taking courses in Drama at Berkeley, and she wore a bare-shouldered, green Taffeta frock that First Lady Frances Cleveland had made so popular. She had a great affinity with Mrs. Cleveland, as they were both twenty-one, and they shared many of the same values about Women's Rights and the fair treatment of Negroes.

Her brother, seventeen-year-old David Milton, who was kidnapped during their mother's most recent case in Washington D.

C., had an impeccable taste in female attire, and he helped her select it. Since he was now allowed to wear dresses around the mansion, Trella trusted Dr. McFarland, the family alienist's modern approach to her brother's psychological well being.

The chubby man standing on the front porch was a stranger. He wore a gentleman's brown derby, a matching extra-large corduroy suit, white shirt, and red silk necktie, and his shoes were the latest spats or gaiters from England. He spoke in an erudite manner, as he brought his right hand up to his derby's brim to salute her.

"Good morning, madam. Is this the residence of Mrs. Clara Shortridge Foltz, Attorney-at-Law? My name is Aloysius Xavier Farmer. I would like to speak with her concerning an important legal matter."

Trella smiled. She knew her mother would be pleased at the prospect of a new client. Without the largesse of Mrs. Hopkins, most of her money now had to be earned from her law practice. The detective side of things would have to wait.

"Why certainly, Mr. Farmer. Please come in. I can go up and inform my mother. I don't believe she is occupied at present." She waved the portly gentleman into the foyer, where she took his hat and hung it on the mahogany rack in the corner.

"Your place is very similar to my own. I live up the road at Twelve Nob Hill. Perhaps we had the same architect?"

Trella watched, as Mr. Farmer's eyes scanned the parlor. Ah Toy's art collection, both paintings and sculptures, covered the walls and filled a variety of strategically positioned *Feng Shui* locations. They accented the Oriental furniture: sofas, lamps, tables, and chairs.

The sunshine was streaming into the room from the bay window, as the red drapes were pulled back. Farmer nodded and began to strut around the room, taking in the décor. She watched, as his eyebrows rose with his wrinkled forehead, and he took in the view. His voluminous frame and ruddy facial features reminded her of John Bunny, the stage actor and comedian. He had recently appeared at Berkeley's campus theater as Fallstaff in *The Merry*

Wives of Windsor. Farmer's wide mouth, rather bulbous and veined nose, and three chins made her smile, remembering Fallstaff's antics. His lamb chop sideburns were dark-brown, the same color as his neatly parted, rather wispy hair. She guessed he was in his early forties.

"Did you live in China?" Mr. Farmer inquired, holding up a Ming vase and studying its blue dragon design.

"No. We have friends who came from China. The owner of this house, in fact, collects art and creates it as well. I shall go up to tell mother you're here. Please make yourself comfortable."

He nodded at her, and she turned around and walked over to the stairs. She noticed the morning's *Chronicle* lying on the small table next to the balustrade. The headline read: *Aloysius Farmer, the Abortifacient King, Sued!* So that's why he was looking for legal assistance. She picked up the paper, tucked it under her arm, and proceeded up the stairs.

Clara's office door was open. Trella tossed the newspaper onto her desk. "He's downstairs. Do you believe it proper to aid such a scandalous bounder? We don't need money *that* badly, do we?"

Her mother turned from her typewriter to glance at what she dropped on the desk. Noting the front page headline, she picked up the paper and began to read the story.

"As I've always taught you, my dear, prejudgement is the root word for prejudice. Once a mind has made a conclusion based upon rumor or even from personal experience, the path toward finding the real truth has been obstructed."

"Yes, mother. But your poor women's abortionist is both fat and sassy. He is downstairs waiting for your unbiased wisdom. I'm afraid I have already prejudged him as being Fallstaff, but you know how I can become overly dramatic. I shall never learn how to become the cold and calculating lawyer, I am afraid. Like you and Laura."

Clara looked up from the newspaper. Her eyes were clear and hazel blue, and she was wearing her usual formal attire, a navy ruffled affair, her neck buttoned up to her chin with a cameo, her auburn hair wound up in an old woman's Victorian coiffure, plumping out in the back like the large bustle she wore beneath her dress when working.

Trella waited. Clara finally looked up again.

"The gentleman is being sued by representatives of eighty various public and private groups, headed by the San Francisco Protestant Orphan Asylum, the first such establishment on the Pacific Coast, founded in 1851. It states that the plaintiffs are seeking damages of two hundred fifty thousand dollars. The charges are undisclosed."

"Now I see why you're interested," Trella said, scowling down at Clara. "But why not be on the accusing side of things?"

"The facts are that Mr. Farmer's daughter, who happens to be of half-Navajo heritage, named her father as the sire of her baby, before she tragically expired inside the residential clinic of Chinatown midwife, Mrs. Honora Fulbright. Under the law, because death bed statements are held to be true statements, Mr. Farmer has been named the father. Furthermore, as we in this suffragist household are quite aware, women and children are still considered chattel under our present laws."

"I know. Property. Can't vote. Can't make a contract or own property. Continue." Her sarcasm was purposeful, as the gentleman downstairs was probably capsizing Ah Toy's artwork with his stomach.

"The result is that the midwife has been arrested for manslaughter, and, because of the deathbed statement, Mr. Farmer's business is now in jeopardy. I shall now go down to discuss this further with our possible client. Please precede me, Trella, I need to make a case file for him."

"A case file? How can you be so certain he will accept? Also, why are you accepting *him*? His daughter was sixteen. She's dead. He raped her." She crossed her chest with her fists. "Would you represent a man who raped me? Just because he had a fortune?"

"Once more, you jump to awkward and inappropriate analogies. Each case has its own facts and its own human actors. These must be applied to the laws we have and not to the laws we think we should have. I shall meet you downstairs."

Trella was seated on the fringed red sofa with the giant golden dragon decorating the back. When Clara came down the stairs, she watched Mr. Farmer, who was wedged into one of the broad-backed yellow chairs near the fireplace, rise to a standing position with great difficulty.

Clara, she knew, would be all business, and she was. She shook his hand forcefully, the new case folder clutched under her left arm.

"Mr. Farmer, I am so sorry for your loss. It is times like these that family becomes a steady rock of support. I trust yours is assisting you to weather the emotional difficulties these incidents can bring? Please, let's go into the library, where I can take notes, and you can bring forth some clarity about what you might need."

"Certainly," he said, and they both began to walk toward the library, on the right, at the far end of the parlor.

The door chimes rang. Trella nodded to her mother. "I shall answer it," she said, rushing toward the front door.

This time it was the familiar face of her mother's partner and personal friend, Laura de Force Gordon. As usual, she wore what she termed her "lawyer for the people" uniform. A black dress, no bustle, with a gray bowed neckerchief, no hat, and black boots. She was eleven years her mother's senior, at forty-nine, yet her clothing was more suitable to an undertaker's matron, Trella thought, as she waved her inside.

"Trella, you won't believe who came to my office this morning," she began, striding into the parlor. "I am going to defend one of the most strident suffragettes in this community. As you may be aware, Mrs. Honora Fulbright assists women who have chosen to end an unwanted pregnancy. As it so happens, I believe in the right of a woman to choose when to bring a child into this world, as the community and the husband should not hold power over the female anatomy, especially when it concerns the woman's health, safety, privacy and financial instability."

"That is quite the coincidence, you see, because mother is presently in private consultation with the wealthy rapist who caused your Mrs. Fulbright to be accused of manslaughter." She smiled.

"Although the word, I would wager, could best be termed womanslaughter. Of course, under the law, do we also include the fetus as a victim? If that's the case, then we need to know its gender as well, do we not? The newspaper said the teenaged victim and would-be mother's name is Penelope Farmer. I trust she might be the Grimm's Fairy Tale version of all those farmer's daughter jokes, no?" She chuckled.

Laura frowned. "I'm afraid Clara may be right about your sarcastic manners. You will never make a decent lawyer if you presume that attitude."

She walked over to the dragon sofa and sat down. She patted the cushion next to her. "Please, attorney Gordon. Be seated. I shall cease and desist my sarcastic demeanor. Tell me about your new case."

Laura smiled and joined her. "I am also a dramatist, believe it or not, and I try to follow the Bard's proclamation about the world being a stage. You are probably stating what our public is now thinking, so I shall take your criticisms as representative of what will, most likely, soon be coming at me in the form of uneducated invective."

"Yes. But not with the cultured vocabulary that you are using," she pointed out. "Your client will be called a baby killer and murderess. And you? Perhaps the Devil's own attorney sent to defend her?"

It was Laura's turn to chuckle, but her lips remained firm. "I don't mean to haggle, but I would assume your critique extends to your mother. She is about to defend the living Satan in this case, is she not?"

She nodded. "Yes. I was already chastised for my critique, but my value seems to be in becoming what you attorneys call a 'devil's advocate,' so perhaps there is some salvation for me yet. Please continue with the armchair defense of this new client of yours."

"I cannot tell you much, as my attorney-client privilege is presently in effect. However, since the press has already been buzzing around the facts at hand, I can tell you my more general stratagem." Laura pushed a lock of black hair from her forehead.

Trella envied the woman's impetuousness. She was so unlike her mother, who used her feminine wiles to throw the opponent off-guard. Laura came at her opposition like a bull defending his herd.

"Let me hear your plan. I am certain you have an excellent one," she said.

"As you and I know, the criminal justice system has made the act of aborting a fetus a crime, but not many cases have been pursued beyond manslaughter because of the very difficult *mens rea* of deliberate intent that must be proved. However, this case has been chosen as a cause celebre for the American Medical Association. Thus, according to the newspapers, I shall be contending with a professional witness. Dr. Horatio Storer will be the State's leading expert." Laura scowled. "Not only must I defend Mrs. Fulbright's actions in order to prove that Miss Farmer died from a spontaneous miscarriage that caused hemorrhaging, and not from Fulbright's negligence, I must also address Dr. Storer's accusations that any type of abortion is placing *any* pregnant female's life in immediate danger."

"I know you and mother differ on this. Whereas you are a socialist who believes in the collective rights of women to choose to have an abortion, mother tends to side with other suffragists, like Mrs. Anthony and Mrs. Stanton. They believe the act of abortion to be a mortal sin, and that one must first address the problems of women's rights and poverty before allowing prostitutes and other poor women to place their bodies at risk simply because they may be inconvenienced. Many suffragists say women die at the rate of thirty percent from surgeries and abortifacients." She was estimating her facts from what her mother had told her, but she wanted to play the good advocate.

"Don't you see? That's the point. I plan to refute this plan of the prosecution to make the case about morality and sin. Our Constitution freed the slaves because they were deprived of their rights. Women, of all races, were not given that same privilege. If they put Storer on the stand to advocate his plan to force women to have all their children in his hospitals, then I shall rebut him by showing how forcing women to have children is a violation of personal privacy. Women, as citizens, should have the same constitutional protection as men and freed male slaves under the Fourteenth Amendment. The State, by forcing women to have children, is depriving them, without any trial, from having a chance at a healthy life, the liberty to freely choose when and with whom they can become pregnant, and the personal property that they might have earned had they not been forced to stay at home in order to raise these children."

She knew her mother's favorite rebuttal to this argument, so she decided to use it.

"However, the abortionist is often a profiteering scoundrel. Remember Madame Restell, in New York City? Since many of her clientele were from the privileged class, often married to Wall Street tycoons and other merchants, she would use the privacy issue to her advantage. She secured many so-called 'loans' from former patients, which were never returned. This amounted to nothing less than blackmail."

Laura nodded, but her frown showed she was ready with a rejoinder.

"Again, you have your mother's naivety in these matters. I contend that it is the very illegality of abortion which makes the practice susceptible to avarice. If we allow men in the medical profession, the so-called 'regulars,' like Dr. Storer, to gain control over women's reproductive rights, then the greedy exploiters like Restell will thrive. Only when women have legal control over their wombs will justice ever be served!" Laura raised her fist in the air.

"But what is your societal argument for this grand defense of women's rights?" She leaned forward in suspense. She knew this was Laura's first-ever case concerning this controversial topic.

"Thank you for asking. Before the industrialization of America, in the Seventeenth and Eighteenth Centuries, women took care of family planning legally, in their own ways. Men did not intervene because women were protected by a wider support group of other women. When the cities began to isolate and separate men and women, these protections of privacy and female support fell apart, and women began to be exploited—both at work and in the bedroom. I therefore contend that the pregnant woman of today has become a victim of both the mental pressure of industrial growth and the wanton greed of male lust. These males have now turned on their women to force them into pregnancies that they cannot afford because of their legal and economic isolation and victimization."

Trella stood up. Her mother was coming out of the library with her new client, Mr. Farmer. She was smiling and nodding her head at something the gentleman was saying.

She watched Laura carefully. The attorney slowly rose to her feet, her eyes riveted upon Clara, as if her friend were strolling in Golden Gate Park with Rasputin.

"Ah, Mr. Farmer, I want you to meet my best friend and legal partner, Laura de Force Gordon. Laura, this is Aloysius Farmer. He lives just a few doors down from us. Our abodes share the same architectural design, it seems, although our décor has more of a transcontinental flavor."

The fat John Bunny doppelgänger smiled, his head nodding toward Laura. "I have agreed to purchase two of the paintings done by the owner, Miss Ah Toy. Have you purchased any of these fine works of art for your own pleasure, Miss Gordon?"

Trella noticed Laura's tight-lipped grin. "No, I am afraid my small apartment on Market Street behind my office barely has room for furniture and me. In fact, most of my clients are poor women who are really not interested in how much artwork I have accumulated on my walls. They simply want to stay out of prison."

She now understood that the rhetorical line was being drawn in the sand between her mother and Laura. Their competition would not cease until these two trials ended, one way or another.

"I completely understand. My clients are also women who are forced to take medicines simply because they cannot afford costlier yet perhaps much better surgical procedures. I just wish my daughter had come to me before taking matters into her own hands, when she became pregnant."

The crocodile tears rolled down his cheeks, and she

imagined what a pig would look like if he were to cry. Dear Penny had accused him of being the father, of course, and this fact was quite unnerving.

He turned to address her. "Trella? I hope your thespian pursuits continue onto the stage. Mrs. Foltz tells me your brother, David, also has a love for acting. He is friends with Sarah Bernhardt. I tried to get Penny, my poor daughter, interested in the more cultured aspirations, as she did have a flair for the dramatic. Yet, as I explained to my new attorney, your mother, she was increasingly becoming ill with superstitions that only her mother, a Native Navajo, could have addressed."

"Thank you, Mr. Farmer. As my mother often remarks about her clients, you are now considered part of the family." She was thinking the opposite sentiment. Although she did realize the entire family would certainly be getting involved in his personal affairs as the trial played itself out.

"Good. Well, I am off to take care of business matters in the city. Thank goodness for our modern cable car network in San Francisco. They even have seats that can hold fellows of my wide girth."

She watched as he waddled to the door, took his derby off the coat rack, placed it on his head, and waited patiently until she opened the door for him. When the door was opened, he stepped out onto the porch and into the morning sunshine. Her mother stood behind her, and they both waved, as he awkwardly trundled his way down the steps and out toward California Street.

When she closed the door, she knew what was going to ensue, and she wouldn't have missed it for the world. Arguments between Laura and her mother were like watching a lioness confront an armadillo. Laura was constantly probing, stalking her prey in a crouch, testing, with her claws, the strength of the armadillo's ironclad and passive-aggressive shield of many-layered defenses, ready to bite into her mother the moment she found a frail one.

"Please. Do not start in, Laura. Let me tell you something before your invective begins to seethe from your mouth like lather." Laura circled her mother, and Clara kept moving to follow Laura's ever-widening arc inside the parlor. Trella said a prayer for Ah Toy's expensive standing sculptures from the Fifth Century in Southern China, one of which, a tall Goddess Mazu, Laura was now fingering as she strode along the carpet.

"The crux at the core of both of our cases is Penelope Farmer, is it not?" Laura probed.

She knew her mother's usual deductive logic would establish the argument, if that's what it was to be. Clara also knew Laura preferred to get to heart of a matter, so that's what she was giving her friend. For the moment, Clara remained silent.

"I plan to interview the entire staff of the Farmer mansion. Especially Mrs. Crutchfield, the girl's tutor. I need to know what she was reading, what her mental health was like, and of what her daily diet consisted." Laura nodded to herself, as if she were mentally checking off a list.

"Yes! In fact, I am going to be going even further in that direction. I will interview both Penelope and her mother, Haseya."

Both she and Laura stared fixedly at Clara.

"They are both dead. Are you joking?" Laura said.

Trella suddenly knew the answer. "Adeline," she blurted out.

Her mother nodded. "Yes. My future daughter-in-law, Adeline Quantrill, may be able to communicate with the past or present incarnation of one or both of these women. I plan to seek that information and possibly use it against the representatives of these private and public so-called 'philanthropic' organizations. We both know what they want, and it's not too different from what we discovered at the Stockton State Insane Asylum. These institutions often prey upon and profit from the public's sins and the unwanted children of those sins."

Laura shook her head until her curled black tresses whipped against her cheeks. "Perhaps I should have you committed back into the asylum. No court will ever accept testimony based upon the words of a spiritualist."

"Perhaps. And perhaps not. If I have a person who can vouch for its veracity, and then back it up with interviews of the participating parties, such as the staff, and your client, Mrs.

Fulbright." Clara smiled.

"My client? She is being prosecuted for manslaughter!" Laura was turning red.

"That doesn't mean the judge will prevent her from testifying in my civil trial. She is innocent until proven guilty, remember? Also, there is one suffragette I have in mind, who presently resides in the English lap of luxury. Like you, she once made her money as a spiritualist, and she came under the personal patronage of one Mr. Cornelius Vanderbilt of New York, where she and her sister learned how to make *real* money. On Wall Street."

Laura gasped. "The Scarlet Sisters? Victoria and Tennessee Claflin?"

Clara nodded. She had never seen her mother so full of mirth. "Absolutely! Not only can they verify the efficacy of communicating with the afterlife, they can astound these men with the philosophy and politics of women and what they can do when they have rights. As a presidential candidate in 1872, Victoria can also give these male jurors some insight into national politics."

Laura was beginning to understand the possible consequences. "I see. Well then, as we are partners, Mrs. Foltz, then you would not have any problem lending me their expertise in my own case. I am thinking of teaching my jurors about their philosophy of Free Love."

Her mother laughed. "Of course, Laura! The international press will be haunting those court rooms like the ghosts of Penny and Haseya Farmer."

"Bow-wow-wow-yip-yip-yowee!"

Coming from just outside Toy mansion, perhaps even on the porch, the three women could hear the coyote's song. Trella knew the mystical symbolism of that call, and she realized it would be only a few days before she understood its actual importance.

Chapter 3: Deep Discovery

The Farmer Mansion, Twelve Nob Hill, San Francisco, June 24, 1887.

C lara had her discovery list of possible witnesses prepared. The initial three were employed by her client, Aloysius Farmer. With their new telephone installed, she was able to call ahead to inform them of her visit. Mrs. Althea Crutchfield told her she would be at the mansion at ten, so she was going to first ask questions of the two live-in staff members, the housekeeper, Madeline O'Rourke, and the chauffeur, Edward Barnes.

As this was a civil trial, the burden of proof for the plaintiff was not as stringent. They must prove with a "preponderance of evidence" rather than "beyond any reasonable doubt." It was the quality of said evidence that was of utmost importance and not the quantity. After reading the written accusations against her client, she was going to begin by pursuing two avenues of defense. The opposition was attempting to prove a "wrongful death," so she needed to gather discovery evidence to counter whatever proof the plaintiff had. As Laura Gordon pointed out, in a different, more just world, Farmer would be prosecuted for rape and manslaughter, but the real world was run by men. Therefore, Laura was defending the woman being accused in criminal court, the midwife, Mrs. Fulbright.

Because of the two hundred fifty thousand dollars being sought after in damages, the charge being made was one of negligence, even though Penelope's confession named Mr. Farmer as the parent of the deceased child. Therefore, the plaintiff would need to prove all three elements required in a negligence civil case, which are: duty of care, a breach of that duty, and proving that Mr. Farmer's actions directly caused the deaths of his daughter and her child in the womb.

Since they already had the deathbed statement of the victim, Penelope Farmer, naming her client as the father, one avenue she thought might be possible would be to prove that Penelope's declaration was nullified because of her mental state when she made it. In other words, she needed to explore whether or not the girl was mentally ill and was not aware of what she was doing, and, most especially, with whom she was doing it. That was her first avenue of discovery. Dr. Andrew McFarland, with whom she had worked during the Stockton Insane Asylum and Supreme Court assassination cases, had agreed to work with her on this case, even though he could not examine the deceased girl. McFarland told her if she could get enough information about her behavior before the abortion from the father and others, then he could make some educated assumptions that she might use in court. Of course, there were also the psychic powers of Adeline, which she planned to use as a way to introduce the Navajo and Spiritualist links to this unique case.

Her second avenue was to use the testimony of Victoria and Tennessee Claflin to show the jury why organizations represented by the plaintiff want to profit from women who seek illegal abortions. These women are too poor to afford children, so the organizations are able to take these orphans in and then reap a bounty from selling the babies they have on the open market to parents who cannot have children.

In addition, they use these children as cheap labor, especially when they are immigrants, coloreds, or the destitute whites. In order to tantalize the press and the jury with the spirit world, she would use Adeline to channel Penelope Farmer and her mother. The Claflin sisters could then testify about how Spiritualism serves as a sounding board for women's rights in a world where men rule every other conventional religious pulpit.

This tactic would refute the plaintiff's attempt to show Mr. Farmer as the cause of the death of his daughter. Instead, she would demonstrate how he had been following the law all along and that it was the society, which forces women to seek abortions because they are pressured by conventional religious beliefs, and the profit motive of the ones who seek to benefit from live births of unwanted children. To accomplish this plan, she would use the Claflin sisters to help her investigate the plaintiff's representative organization,

Edgewood, the San Francisco Protestant Asylum, the oldest such entity. This was the group that filed the lawsuit in the first place. She learned from Captain Isaiah Lees, her lover, that one stood the best chance at finding scandal by interviewing those who knew where the money was taken in and how it was handled.

She already knew that these private and public orphanages were tax-exempt, even though the State had no direct supervisorial role over their daily activities. The State of California, because of its history of a nomadic and mostly male population, developed a very *laissez-faire* attitude toward the welfare of miscreants and the poor. In effect, these orphanages were very similar to the State Insane Asylums and other public hospitals, and she had a great deal of experience with those entities, especially with the Stockton State Insane Asylum.

She also knew that in addition to the money they were getting from private, religious subscriptions and donations from the wealthy of San Francisco, many of them were directly subsidized by the State. These organizations were able to make money from their orphans by placing them into indentured servitude until the age of 21, for males, and 18, for females. That made for quite a lot of money coming into these private and incorporated "welfare" organizations. They collected the children's wages, a state subsidy, and a tax-free income, in return for the child's limited education, food, clothing and shelter.

The front entrance had big Greek columns and a wide portico, with brick steps leading up to the door. They had a garden out front with bronze fencing on three sides. As she walked up the forty-five steps leading to the porch, she was thinking about the questions she would ask. She already knew the basics about the three people, as Mr. Farmer had given her the details during his recent visit. Her main purpose was to find out if they had any inside information about the mother and daughter who had lived here.

Mrs. O'Rourke answered the door, and Mr. Barnes was already waiting in the kitchen. Madeline O'Rourke had worked for Farmer for the past six years, and she was older, sixty-two, with a heavy-set frame and a height of five-two. Her white-laced blouse was open at the collar, and a large crucifix dangled between her ample bosoms. Her black skirt was bell-shaped from wide, child-bearing hips, and her maid's cap was also black.

After she sat down, and opened her notepad, she discovered from the chauffer, who had worked for Mr. Farmer for twelve years, that the mansion was constructed by the same architect, Augustus Laver. Laver also designed Ah Toy's home and the James Clair Flood mansion near the top of Nob Hill. All three homes were replica two-story Brownstones meant to emulate the East Coast mansions of the wealthy. Whereas most of the mansions on Nob Hill, including the Hopkins mansion, were made of wood, these three homes were made of stone masonry.

"Mr. Farmer likes to take the cable car down California to his office on Market, but I take him to his social functions in other parts of the city."

Mr. Barnes was a thin, fifty-eight-year-old Negro, about five feet, eight inches tall, and he wore the usual black gabardines, brass buttons shaped in a triangular pattern on the front of his jacket, with matching cap and visor. He had a thin mustache and a personable smile.

"As you both are probably aware, I am representing your employer in a civil lawsuit brought against him by a collection of San Francisco orphan homes and charities. I need to know more information about the ladies of the house. I know that Penelope's mother, Haseya, was a Navajo tribal member. She died three years ago from consumption. Were either of you here when she was ill?"

They both nodded, but Madeline looked down at her freckled hands and sighed.

"Mrs. O'Rourke? Did you observe anything out of the ordinary between any of the family members?"

She was expecting the usual tale of emotional temper tantrums and perhaps personal attacks. She was hoping there weren't visits to Penelope's room by Mr. Farmer.

"The most ungodly mischief I ever seen! I go to bed at ten, and these walls are thick. Never heard a peep before that night. But when the mother came down with consumption, after they got back from their Arizona visit to her tribe, I began to hear a strange barking at night. Then, over the next few nights, I could hear someone thrashing around inside the mother's room next-door. On the third night, I opened my bedroom door a crack, to look out, you know?"

She made the sign of the cross.

"And I seen the little lass race down the hall toward me. Like her black hair was on fire. She was crouched over, her head raised up. She stopped in her tracks. And then she howled. Never seen or heard the likes of it before. When I told her about it the next day, she just smiled at me, but she never spoke another word from that day forward. Her mother died three days later."

Mr. Barnes nodded. "She's right about the girl not talking. Even Mrs. Crutchfield complained about the girl being mum. I live in the colored section of the city, so I don't know about what happens here at night. The girl was most always in the library, during the day. I do know that. I did take them all shopping after they returned from Arizona."

"Did you see any signs the girl was pregnant? Was anything ever mentioned?" She wanted to probe the areas in which the plaintiff might be interested.

"No. I'm not married, so I wouldn't know what to look for," Barnes said.

Mrs. O'Rourke raised her hand, as if she were in school. "Me and my three girls all had children, and we all got the morning sickness. Penelope had it too. I seen her heave up her toes many times. She even vomited on the day she left to see Mrs. Fulbright."

That was interesting. Did O'Rourke know about the abortionist?

"How did you know she was going to see Mrs. Fulbright?"

The maid smiled. "Oh, I never knew about it then. I read about it in the paper. I put two and two together afterwards. When she died. At the time, I thought little Penny was ill because of her mother's death. If I known she was going to get her baby murdered . . ." she again made the sign of the cross. "That Fulbright woman should be hanged! It's a mortal sin what she does. Jesus preserve us all!"

That brought up an interesting dilemma she wanted to now investigate.

"Does either of you know how Mr. Farmer makes his income?"

They both began to fidget in their chairs.

"Well?" Her voice was adamant.

"Mr. Farmer told us both about his business when we first began to work here. Because of the demonstrators who came to visit almost every month," Barnes said.

"And Mr. Farmer ain't no abortionist! He's a Protestant, but he's no abortionist. He showed us the label that goes on each bottle of Dr. Goody's Female medicine he sells. It says, in all capital letters NOT FOR PREGNANT WOMEN," Mrs. O'Rourke explained, nodding her head for emphasis.

"It's a medication to help women have better menstrual flows, is how he explained it," Barnes said. "He told us these demonstrators were riled up by what that U. S. Postal Inspector said."

"Anthony Comstock?" She knew this gentleman very well. He was certain to be one of the plaintiff's main witnesses.

"That's him. Mr. Farmer says that Comstockery is making women get all kinds of female diseases that can be prevented by what my boss sells. People demonstrate when some ignorant woman takes Dr. Goody's potions after they get pregnant. Boss calls it 'drinking the pennyroyal tea.' That's akin to suicide."

She was getting all her client's products analyzed by a chemist. They were certain to become a major focus during the trial. Pennyroyal, she knew, was a main ingredient in the female menstrual potion Farmer sold, and Clara knew it would be a major bone of contention. In her cursory research, she knew that for hundreds of years, before surgery was available to women, they used pennyroyal to prevent pregnancy. It was an unassuming flower, with its small, pointed, lavender petals cupped by deep green leaves. Pennyroyal flowers grew in tiny clusters that thread a single, delicate stem. In small doses, it helps to improve menstrual flow. She also knew that at higher doses it can also kill.

"Mrs. Foltz?" A tall woman wearing spectacles and a dark gray dress with medium bustle entered the kitchen. She stood at the head of the table, at attention, surveying everyone with an overbearing manner. Her brown hair, rolled into a bun, was streaked with gray, and she had the studious, pursed lips of a teacher.

"Yes, Mrs. Crutchfield. I am so happy you could come. Won't you be seated?"

Clara knew the woman was fifty-two, a mother of three, who had served as a private tutor for fifteen years. Before that she was a principal at a girls' academy in San Jose for ten years. Aloysius Farmer said he hired her because she was an expert at teaching young girls the True Woman Method. Mr. Farmer and Trella Evelyn informed her that this curriculum gave daughters of the wealthy elite the basic skills they needed to run a household. The practical skills of mathematics, reading, and writing. She must also, at all times, be subservient to the male head of the household and to the same patriarchy that controlled all of society.

The tutor used a handkerchief to wipe off the seat of the kitchen chair before she sat down. She frowned at Mr. Barnes and Mrs. O'Rourke.

"Do you mind? I have some private information to share with Mrs. Foltz."

Clara stood up to shake hands with the two regular employees.

"Thank you for your assistance," she said.

All the other staff were day workers who left the mansion after their chores were completed. What she needed to know about Penelope Farmer could possibly be given to her by the tutor now sitting across from her.

"As you know, Mrs. Crutchfield, I am defending Mr. Farmer. I have been a teacher in my early years, so I am very sympathetic to your duties. I need to know the truth about what his daughter was doing, as you can be a very important resource for my defense." She smiled at the teacher. "What is this personal information you have for me?"

The tutor nodded slowly. "I understand. I must be frank with you, Mrs. Foltz. I am not a person who necessarily believes what she teaches. Were you a public school teacher?"

"Yes. In Iowa and Indiana." She was interested in this line of thought. It might mean Crutchfield had a better insight into the girl's character than she had initially expected.

"As you must know, teaching in the public environment requires an adherence to established policies. When I became principal in San Jose, I suddenly had to learn the private sector's practices. In the private sector, for the most part, you do what the parents require."

"I am quite familiar with the differences. My daughter attends a public university, and I have had personal dealings with Mr. Leland Stanford and his policies at that private university." She did not want to discuss the problems she had with Stanford's support of Eugenics and her recent experiences at the Stockton State Insane Asylum.

"I am an avowed suffragist. What I teach to these wealthy elites is simply pecuniary in nature. I can make more money. What I have to tell you about Penelope and her family is because I am a supporter of women's rights." She took out a sheet of paper from her gray handbag, unfolded it on the table, and ran a forefinger down a list she had compiled.

"Thank you for the honesty. Although I am defending your employer, I still want to know the truth. If there have been illegal activities going on, then I am bound by legal ethics to report them to the proper authorities."

She was hoping she could continue in her defense of Mr. Farmer, as she also needed the money.

"It all began when the family returned from Arizona. The mother, as you know, was Navajo. Despite what Mr. Farmer instructed me to do, I could not get Penelope to learn anything unless I agreed to listen to the two females' demands concerning what the tribe believes. Mrs. Farmer, who spoke no English, was translated by the girl, and I have made a list of their four most important beliefs, so you can see for yourself why I am now concerned."

"Please. Illuminate me."

She lifted her pencil, ready to write it down on the pad.

"First of all, the Navajo people, the Diné, pass through three different worlds before emerging into this world, the Fourth World, or Glittering World. The Diné believe there are two classes of beings: the Earth People and the Holy People. The Holy People are believed to have the power to aid or harm the Earth People. Since Earth People of the Diné are an integral part of the universe, they must do everything they can to maintain harmony or balance on Mother Earth."

"I can see how your True Woman curricula would differ with these beliefs. There is no mention of male or female in this Navajo legend."

She was very intrigued. She might use this information as a possible reason why Penelope would become mentally confused or not know the consequence of her own actions.

"Yes. Secondly, the four directions are represented by four colors: White Shell represents the east, Turquoise the south, Yellow Abalone the west, and Jet Black the north. In the Navajo culture there are four directions, four seasons, the first four clans and four colors that are associated with the four sacred mountains. In most Navajo rituals there are four songs and multiples thereof, as well as Navajo wedding basket and many other symbolic uses of four."

"And you have four items on your list. I assume we are now reaching the important practices," she guessed.

"Indeed, we are. When the mother, Haseya, was diagnosed with fatal consumption, she called in the Medicine Man from her tribe. Because I was charged with Penelope's education, I was allowed to listen to what the holy man told her. He said the disease she had was because of a curse placed on the family from a Holy person visiting from one of the three other worlds."

"What did they do to cause this curse?" She wrote down the facts and leaned forward in expectation.

"He told them Mr. Farmer was an Earth Person who was going against the harmony of Mother Earth in the Glittering World. He told Haseya and Dezba, which is the girl's tribal name, that they had to use their powers as *yee naaldooshii* to put Aloysius back on a harmonious path."

"What do those words mean? What were their powers?" She wanted a term she could better describe to a jury.

"Dezba means war. *Yee naaldooshii* means skinwalkers, as the mother later explained to me. Skinwalkers are Holy people who can change into an animal to protect the sacred ancestral traditions."

"Very interesting. Women who protect the tribal law. Is there anything else?" She wrote down the term "skinwalker" and circled it.

"Yes. They were told they must lose their lives, if need be, to protect the harmony. However, in retribution, four evil Earth people in the Glittering World would eventually lose their lives."

"In retribution? You mean, after Hasaya and Dezba died?" This was special information to perhaps be explored by psychic Adeline Quantrill.

"Yes. Two evil Earth people must die for each Holy skinwalker who dies. You see, according to the Medicine Man, the animal possession abilities of skinwalker witches do not die with their bodies. They continue in the Glittering World as spirit advocates for the Diné."

"Advocates? Sounds almost like a lawyer. Or ghosts. Do you mean these spirit entities will kill people?" She wanted some place to hang her rhetorical hat.

"Yes. Kill. Now I am going to tell you the most frightening experience that I've ever had in my life—both in and out of a classroom filled with maniacal students. It happened after Mrs. Farmer passed away from the curse, or from the consumption, whichever culture is your preference."

It was Mrs. Crutchfield's turn to lean forward. The lenses in her spectacles reflected the light beaming down from the new electric bulb installed inside the small overhead chandelier. It was as if some kind of spiritual presence had entered her brain from another world.

Clara shivered involuntarily. "Go on. I'm listening," she said.

The entire kitchen seemed to get warmer. The stove was not

on. The electric light could not emit that much heat. She believed a spiritual presence had entered them both, as a warning.

"After the funeral, Penny began to take over all the household duties. She became officious, organized and efficient, just like her mother. However, she also did all of this the way her mother had done it. Without speaking."

"She never spoke to anybody?" She wrote it down. It validated what Mrs. O'Rourke had told her.

"She did not speak. I obviously could not teach her any lessons. She became obsessed. And then, the week she left the house to go to the midwife in Chinatown, she began to wear her mother's clothing. And, then came the most provoking change. I saw her face and mannerisms transform into the exact duplicate of Haseya Farmer."

"Are you certain? Were you tired or under any pressure at the time?" She wanted a sworn statement, as she predicted her opponent's questioning the woman's mental state.

"I was leaving the house, and she turned toward me after coming out of the master bedroom. When I addressed her, she spoke to me for the first time in weeks. She said exactly what her mother always said, *Hágoónee*. The Navajo never says goodbye. She says 'all right then.' I had no answer, of course. I was too dumbfounded to reply."

"Are you willing to testify to this under oath, Mrs. Crutchfield? I will need the exact date and time as well."

She could take the risk to convince a jury. This testimony would combine well with her other excursions into the unknown. Her father, also a lawyer, always told her that taking chances with stories was far more effective with a jury than tedious expert testimony.

"It was June 20. I remember the time. I gazed at the grandfather clock that stood in the bedroom hall next to her mother's room. The time was 4:04 PM. The fours startled me."

Clara could feel the perspiration run down her back, between her breasts, and over her face. It was like an oven.

The distinct yipping and yapping howl of the coyote caused

them to stand up from their chairs at the kitchen table. Their eyes were wide in expectant fear, as they listened to the continuing cry of the animal. It was coming from outside, but its penetrating song made the room hotter, if that were indeed possible.

"And … that was what I heard from her on the day she became the image of her mother. Her face, in the shadows of early twilight, momentarily transformed into the quivering snout, the flashing teeth, and the howling snarl of a coyote."

Clara moved over to where Mrs. Crutchfield was standing. She took the older woman's hands into her own. She could feel the sweat, and she could feel the tremoring shivers from both of their appendages.

"I must confess to you as well," she whispered.

"What do you mean, confess?" the teacher stared, mesmerized by Clara's hazel eyes.

"I heard the same howl this morning, after Mr. Farmer left my home. How do you suppose these skinwalkers move so fast? Also, how do they kill humans?" She was captured by her own fear, so her questions were coming from the illogical, hot-white core of that same trepidation.

"They run on all fours, and they can run two-hundred miles in one evening. The Medicine Man said that if you accidentally lock eyes with a skinwalker, it can absorb itself into your body and take control of your actions."

Clara tried to make her voice louder, but it came out of her mouth as a squealing sound. "How do they kill?"

"He told us they enchant the powder of corpses and use the substance as a poison dust on victims."

When the lights went out, they both screamed.

Historical Notes

When I worked at Caltech, I understood a very important theory: the past, the present, and the future exist at the same moment. It requires only the proper vehicle in order to travel between them. That "vehicle" is one's mind. If we can invent an actual time machine, for our bodies, that's one thing, and it's probably impossible. But we can invent, using the historical record, which is our human past, a written record of creativity (Historical Fiction). And we can, using the extrapolating method of ingenious fiction, create our possible future (Science Fiction).

I invented historical fiction mysteries in the Portia of the Pacific series because I wanted to create a time machine of the mind. I wanted to blend actual history with a fictional mystery and combine them both with characters who have empathy and courage.

In this, the fourth mystery in my series, *The Angel's Trumpet*, I wish to point out the history as it is juxtaposed with the fictional imagination of my mental time machine. As you read the plot, you can become aware of what is "theoretically" based on fact, and what is "theoretically" based on a creative writer's imagination. Living life in 2019, that task has become very relevant to educated readers.

All of the major characters in this novel are based on actual persons, except for five. 1. Dr. Goodrich Lightfoot (although I did appropriate the Lightfoot family history to serve my fictional purposes). 2. Detective Hubert Abercrombie. 3. Judge Marshal Owens. 4. Eloise Strong. 5. Erin Scully.

As for the historical events, the major event, the assassination of Judge Owens, is complete fiction. The only attempted assassination of a Supreme Court Justice, Stephen Johnson Field, came at the hands of David S. Terry, former Chief Justice of the California Supreme Court. In 1889, Terry was killed by Field's bodyguard in Stockton, California. Terry was angry over a court appeal by Terry's wife, the beautiful Sarah Althea Hill, who was suing silver millionaire, William Sharon, in a matrimony case. Field, when he was a judge in California, had thrown her case against Sharon out of court. Hill was later confined, and died, inside the Stockton State Insane Asylum, which is the setting and focus of my third mystery in the series, *The Stockton Insane Asylum Murder*. Althea Hill does not appear in it.

The setting and historical facts concerning Washington D. C. in 1887 are all based on the historical record. Drugs, such as opium and heroin, were legal and being used regularly by entrepreneurs as "patent medicines" in a variety of advertising and promotional schemes. This is comparable to our current "Opioid Crisis" brought on by corporations who use the same advertising tactics to make billions and to murder over 200,000 United States citizens in a single year. The Angel's Trumpet (Devil's Breath) is a plant used to produce LSD effects and is currently being used by bands of Chinese criminals to turn its victims into willing zombies.

The baseball color barrier was first broken by Moses Fleetwood Walker, a catcher, who was a very educated man. He actually wrote a book about Black Nationalism entitled *Our Home Colony*. His experiences with racism were much more psychologically debilitating than Jackie Robinson's, who was given credit for breaking the race barrier in 1947. Of course, as a black man espousing black nationalism, many of our historians are not kind to him. I hope I gave him some of the credit that was due him.

First Lady Frances Cleveland was quite popular with the American public, and she became the first woman married within the White House to become a celebrity. However, she did differ with her husband, Stephen Grover Cleveland, on many social issues, including the treatment of Negroes.

Sarah Bernhardt, the "Divine Sarah," did make world tours to pay for her mounting debt in France. She was also a philanthropist and a proud Jew. One of the greatest actresses the world has ever enjoyed, she was very open to adventure and new experiences. She fit quite well in my plot and with my main sleuthing characters from San Francisco.

The overall cultural setting of the Gilded Age is very comparable to today's problems. The backlash against the liberal policies of Reconstruction following the Civil War was in full swing, exemplified by the 1883 decision declaring the Civil Rights Act of 1875 null and void. The same thing is happening today, with the war against the liberal 1968 Civil Rights Act. Negroes in the national congress and state legislatures had been cut from 1,500, during the height of Reconstruction in the 1870s, to just five, in the 1880s. Also, the election of Democrat Stephen Grover Cleveland, who believed the government should not give handouts to the people, demonstrated an electorate who was more interested in keeping out immigrants, using the Chinese Exclusion Act as a weapon to do that, and keeping Negroes and women "in their proper places." Also, President Cleveland could see brothels from his White House windows.

His Attorney General, Augustus Garland, is the only cabinet member ever officially censured by Congress. He refused to hand over documents relating to the termination of one his Federal State Attorneys.

Finally, the divide between rich and poor is also comparable, in that only 4,000 mostly white families controlled the majority of the capital and wealth of the United States and its economy. Today, last time I checked, eight white men control over fifty percent of our nation's economy, and that divide is growing exponentially, around the world, every day.

Please join our social page to ask questions of the author.
Facebook.com/portiaofpacific/

ACKNOWLEDGEMENTS

I spent many hours doing the requisite research. I hope the reader enjoys the realistic rendering of the era and its political atmosphere as well as its growing pains. I am a firm believer in the adage of "history repeating itself," and that was the main impetus for creating my series. I suddenly awakened to the fact that I was living inside a modern Gilded Age, and we could learn a lot by going back and seeing how it was for others who were living and dealing with the same kinds of issues and problems. The PBS series, *American Experience*, concerning life in The Gilded Age, also assisted me, as well as the hundreds of articles and books about the Administration of President Grover Cleveland, the life of actress Sarah Bernhardt, and baseball player Moses Fleetwood Walker, which I weaved into my mystery with astute attention to accuracy.

ABOUT THE AUTHOR

James Musgrave's work has been recently featured in *Best New Writing 2011*, Eric Hoffer Book Awards, Hopewell Press, Titusville, N.J. He was semi-finalist in the Black River Chapbook Competition, Fall, 2012. He was also in a Bram Stoker Award Finalist volume of horror fiction, *Beneath the Surface, 13 Shocking Tales of Terror*, Shroud Publishing, San Francisco, CA. His historical mystery series starring Detective Patrick James O'Malley was selected as "featured titles" by the American Library Association's Self-E Program for Independent Authors. The first mystery in that series, *Forevermore*, won the First-Place blue ribbon for Best Historical Mystery, in the Chanticleer International Clue Book Awards, 2013. James lives in San Diego, and is the publisher of EMRE Publishing, LLC.

Sign-up for the Author's Newsletter at emrepublishing.com

www.ingramcontent.com/pod-product-compliance
Lightning Source LLC
Chambersburg PA
CBHW051506170626
46811CB00002B/675